Parting may bring their true feelings to the surface.

"I'll miss you, Darlene. You don't know how much."

Touched, she gave him a hug, and was surprised when he hugged her back tightly. All she could feel was the pressure of their two coats, but his breath was warm on her cheek.

"May I kiss you good-bye?"

She was surprised, but delighted that he asked. "Of course you may, Jake." She kissed his cheek, feeling the day's growth of beard with her lips. Warmth filled her heart; her knees felt weak. She waited with closed eyes for the long-anticipated touch of his lips upon her cheek. He need never know that his kiss meant far more to her than a simple farewell gesture.

To her utter surprise, his return kiss landed on her lips, or nearly. He missed on the first try. Her mouth dropped open just in time for him to find it with his; the unexpected passion of his embrace shocked and thrilled her.

"Jake?" she breathed when he released her.

He caressed her cheek with a trembling hand. "I shouldn't have done that, but. . .you're so sweet! Can you forgive me?"

Still stunned, she could only nod.

"Good-bye, Darlene."

JILL STENGL makes her home in North Carolina with her family. *Finally, Love* is her second inspirational romance novel. The setting is taken from her experiences living on a U.S. Air Force base in England where her husband had been stationed.

Books by Jill Stengl

HEARTSONG PRESENTS
HP197—Eagle Pilot

Finally, Love

Jill Stengl

Heartsong Presents

To my wonderful parents,
Dick and Bobbie Harrison.
I love you, Daddy and Mama.
Thank you with all my heart.

A note from the Author:
I love to hear from my readers! You may write to me at
the following address: **Jill Stengl**
Author Relations
P.O. Box 719
Uhrichsville, OH 44683

All scripture quotations, unless otherwise indicated, are taken
from the HOLY BIBLE, NEW INTERNATIONAL VERSION®.
NIV®. Copyright © 1973, 1978, 1984 by International Bible
Society. Used by permission of Zondervan Publishing House.
All rights reserved.

ISBN 1-57748-063-5

FINALLY, LOVE

Cover illustration by Kay Salem.

PRINTED IN THE U.S.A.

one

It all happened so quickly, Darlene didn't have time to be frightened until after the fact. She had been singing along with her favorite Christian tape, keeping both eyes firmly on the road as her van labored to follow its sharp curves. She saw headlights approaching in the opposite lane, but didn't realize that she would meet the other vehicle nearly head-on in the center of a narrow bridge until it was too late to brake.

Wham! Her van shuddered but continued across the bridge without a pause.

I'm not dead. I'm not wrecked. What on earth happened? On the far side of the bridge Darlene pulled over. Bare branches scraped the left side of the van as she rolled to a stop; the road had no shoulder, or "verge" as it was called here in England.

Oh, great. Now I've scratched up that side of the van, too. For a long moment she sat clutching her chest with her heart pounding and trying not to fly into hysterics. *I told Dad I don't like to drive here! Why does he insist that I drive? I hate it! I hate it!*

In her rearview mirror she saw the taillights of the other vehicle. It had stopped across the bridge, and a figure moved around it in the darkness, evidently looking for damage. Knowing she should do something, Darlene opened the glove compartment. *Where does Dad keep the registration, or, no, wait, maybe it's insurance proof I need? Oh, I don't know!* Grabbing a handful of important-looking papers, she climbed through the van and slid open the side door. With all those bushes in the way, she could never have opened her door.

It took only a glance to determine the damage. The American-built van's passenger side mirror was smashed, though its bracket still held. There were marks on the side window where the mirror had bashed into it before snapping back into place. No other damage was apparent, though it was difficult to tell in the dark.

Footsteps crunched on the road behind her. Shivering with cold and nerves, Darlene turned to face the other driver's wrath.

It was a man.

It would be, she inwardly groaned. Alone at night on a country road with a strange man whose car she had just bashed. Great.

"Are you all right?" It was an American voice, at least.

"Yes. Are you?" She sounded like a scared little girl.

"I'm fine, but my mirror's shot. Looks like yours is too."

"I—I've got insurance information," she volunteered.

"Yeah, I do, too. What would you say happened just now? Could you tell we were going to hit?" He sounded so calm! Darlene felt like throwing up.

"I knew it was going to be close, but by that time it was too late to stop. If I had swerved away, I would have landed in the ditch or hit the bridge railing."

"Same here. Hey, I'm sorry this happened to you. . .I mean, I'm sorry it happened to me, too, but you look so upset. Sure you're all right?"

The van's inside light reflected from his glasses when Darlene glanced up at him and tried to smile. "I think so." She belied her own words by catching a gasping sob, then turned and tried to scramble back into the van, childishly wanting nothing more than to hide her lack of composure. Her foot slipped; she hit her knee on the running board and nearly fell face first into the upholstered seat. Hard hands gripped her shoulders and pulled her upright.

"Whoa, settle down! We can be thankful this was nothing worse than a couple of broken mirrors. I've heard that few Americans make it through an assignment over here without getting a side mirror knocked off. Our vans and trucks are just too big for these narrow English roads. It wasn't anybody's fault!"

He had a nice voice, gentle and mellow. Darlene's eyes flickered over him with sudden interest. He was young, under thirty anyway, and wore a leather flight jacket over a khaki green flight suit. A silver lieutenant's bar shone on his blue flight cap. Darlene's heart suddenly fluttered for a new reason, and she lost her jitters.

"That's better." He reached inside his leather jacket to his flight suit's shoulder pocket for a pen, then unzipped a pocket on the side of his ankle and pulled out his wallet.

Darlene glanced at the papers in her hand, wondering which one had the information he needed.

He scribbled something on the back of a wrinkled business card. "How about we just exchange addresses and phone numbers for now? I don't have anything better than this to write on," he apologized, offering the card. "It's too dark and cold to figure out insurance, and maybe you'd rather I discussed it with your father?"

Darlene relaxed visibly. "Oh, yes, thank you, sir!" She felt him watching while she located a scrap of paper in her purse, wrote on it with a shaking hand, and handed it to him.

He glanced at the card and looked up. "Pleased to meet you, Miss Darlene Althorp."

She looked at his card for the first time. "Mr. Edgewood?" He nodded. "You live in West Row? We live in Holywell Row. I was taking this back way to church, which was probably a stupid thing to do after dark. Come to think of it, I'm going to be awfully late!"

"Church on Tuesday night?"

"It's a Valentine's Day party. I help lead the girls' club at our church."

"I see." He gave her a brief smile. "Hope this hasn't spoiled your evening. I'll be contacting you soon, Miss Althorp."

Darlene arrived late at the party, but Polly Shackleton, the club leader, readily forgave her once she explained. The next few hours were too full of games, songs, and stories for Darlene to give much thought to her late adventure.

Afterward, while helping Polly take down decorations, her thoughts returned to the accident and Mr. Edgewood. *I wonder why he was on the Undley road? It's not on the way between the base and his home. I wonder if he's married? I didn't think to look for a ring.*

"Mission nearly accomplished," Polly interrupted, rolling up a paper tablecloth that was soaked with red punch. "All but the tables. Now, what do you think about a St. Patrick's Day slumber party next month?" She made a fake grin.

Darlene wrinkled her nose and chuckled. "I think you can find another assistant, please! This was fun, but I need a long break before I take on another such project."

"You need time to forget, right?" Polly teased.

Darlene only rolled her eyes and laughed. She adored Polly, who treated her as an equal, though there was nearly ten years' difference in their ages.

"Think they had fun?" Polly asked, brushing dark curls off her forehead.

"They certainly seemed to; my head is still ringing. I wonder if I always talked at top speed and full volume when I was that age."

"Probably. I think it's an inherent trait in little girls," Polly said wryly, bending to sweep crumbs into the dustpan. "Darlene, I can't tell you how much I appreciate having you work with me. When Lisa had to quit as leader, I felt incapable of taking over for her, but with your help I think I'm gonna make it. You know, when I'm with you I don't even think about the difference in our ages. You're quite mature for your age."

Darlene helped Polly turn a table on its side and fold up the legs. The praise pleased her, but she felt unworthy. "I don't feel very mature. That man tonight, the one I crashed with, knew I was just a kid right away."

"Did he? He must have a discerning eye to determine your age so quickly. You seem so grown up."

"Hardly. I nearly started bawling then, and I still feel like it now."

"Of course you do, honey! Any woman would, after a near miss like that. I bet that guy was impressed by your self-control!"

"I doubt it. And how am I gonna tell Dad about this? He'll kill me!"

"Now I know you're exaggerating. Don, angry? That I find hard to imagine."

"He does get mad once in a while, believe it or not." Darlene sat on a folding chair and sighed, running both hands through her long blond hair.

Polly looked sympathetic. "From what you said, Darlene, this accident wasn't your fault. It could have happened to anyone."

"I think I was driving too fast. I mean, I wasn't over the national speed limit, but it was too fast for that dark, winding road. I feel so stupid! I'll have to baby-sit every weekend for the next five years to pay for that mirror. I just know it!"

Polly smiled, losing some of her sympathy. "Don't be silly. Come here and help me fold up this table."

Darlene obeyed, but she still looked glum.

"I know how you feel, honey." Polly's husky voice penetrated the younger girl's gloomy thoughts.

"You do?" Darlene didn't mean to look skeptical, but Polly must have seen the doubt in her eyes. Polly Shackleton was one of the most beautiful women Darlene had ever seen, with masses of curly brown hair, brilliant dark eyes, creamy skin, and a fabulous figure. Newly married to a fighter pilot after a short and stormy courtship, admired by men and women alike, Polly epitomized Darlene's idea of romance and glamour. How could a woman like that ever feel immature or inadequate? "I hate growing up, Polly. I wish I were ten years old again and didn't have to drive."

"Yeah, I know what you mean. Sometimes I feel like a little girl playing grown-up, and I'm afraid I'll be found out eventually. Say, my husband is flying tonight; he won't be home till late. Are your folks expecting you home, or can you stay to talk?"

"I've got time. Dad's in Germany until tomorrow. Mom's home with the boys."

"Let's finish cleaning up, then stop in town for a cup of tea or coffee, all right? I know a pub with a quiet dining room."

They worked much more efficiently after that, and the church was soon spotless. Collecting their purses and bags of craft supplies, the two young women locked up the church building and hurried out to the car park.

"Meet you at the Half Moon Pub."

"I'll follow you there."

Darlene trembled as she climbed into her parents' minivan. Even before tonight's incident she hadn't completely adjusted to driving on the left side of the road, although her family had lived in England for more than six months. Actually, she had never been adept at driving on any side of the road, having obtained her license only weeks before leaving the States. It was a relief to follow Polly to Lakenheath village. She wouldn't think about driving home until the time came.

The two young women lingered over their cups of tea, laughing and chatting, mostly about love and marriage—Polly's marriage. Polly described a few of the trials and joys of life with a fighter pilot. She had only been married since Christmas and found married life surprising in many ways—not all of them happy ways. Still, she was very much in love with her husband and did not regret her hasty marriage.

Darlene drank in every word Polly spoke, longing to emulate her. Peter Shackleton, Polly's husband, wasn't the most handsome or dashing man in the world, but Darlene found any romance fascinating, especially a passionate, whirlwind courtship such as Polly's had been.

"I'm glad Peter was working tonight, because I hate to leave him alone in the evening. Oh, changing the subject, I wanted to ask what you thought of my devotional tonight. Was it too far over the girls' heads?"

Darlene thought for a moment before replying. "It's a difficult concept for children to take in, you know, the idea of giving one's heart to the Lord. That little Julianne Fahner gives all the right answers, but I don't think she understands any of them. It's all rote memorization with her."

Polly stirred her tea, gazing thoughtfully at Darlene. "I was raised in a Christian home, faithfully attended private schools, Sunday school, and church, yet I was an adult before all the head knowledge I had soaked in sank deeper—into my heart. It's a blessing to have Christian training, and I wouldn't give it up for the world, but it took a long time for me to appreciate and apply the knowledge I have. How is your personal relationship with the Lord, Darlene?"

Put on the spot, Darlene didn't want to seem hesitant, so she immediately answered, "Great."

If Polly saw her tension, she didn't let on. "You're blessed, then. Of course, not many people have wonderful parents like yours. It must be fun to be home schooled and spend so much time with your family."

"Oh, yes, it is!" Darlene enthused, feeling herself on safer ground. "I really miss my sister now that she's married, but Mom and I are closer than ever."

"Your mother is so sweet, and your father is a doll." Polly grinned. "You know what I mean."

Darlene smiled back, "Yes, I know what you mean. I think he's adorable."

Adorable. The word started a new chain of thoughts, though Darlene could not have explained why it brought her recent accident to mind. "I wonder if Peter knows the man I collided with tonight. He was a lieutenant, I think."

Polly's brows lifted, but she didn't question the sudden change of topic. "He's in the air force? You didn't tell me that. What's his name?"

"Edgewood." Darlene pulled the card from a side pocket of her purse. "J. K. Edgewood, it says. He was wearing a flight suit, a leather jacket, and a blue cap with a silver bar."

Polly looked thoughtful. "Edgewood. Hmm. It does sound familiar, but I don't think I've met him. Did you happen to notice what patches he had on? I mean, he could have been from RAF Mildenhall, or from any of the squadrons at RAF Lakenheath. Peter's name patch is red with black lettering, and his shoulder patch shows a black panther."

"No, I didn't notice patches. It was too dark. He was very nice, but not real tall. I mean, he's about my height." Darlene sounded wistful.

Polly smiled understandingly. Girlhood crushes were not too distant in her own past. "I'll ask Peter if he knows him."

two

"Weren't you scared to death? Alone at night out in the boonies with a strange man!" Joanna exclaimed. The two girls waited in the choir loft for the morning church service to begin, whispering behind their songbooks.

"It was scary, but not as scary as Dad's face when he saw the mirror and the scratches I put on the van," Darlene admitted ruefully. "Shh, I'll tell you more later."

"Turn in your hymnals to page two forty-one, 'Love Lifted Me.' Page two forty-one!" From the podium Don Althorp glanced at his wife, seated at the piano, and nodded. After Dora's short introduction, he burst into song, " 'I was sinking deep in sin far from the peaceful shore. . .' " The first note wasn't quite right, and he waved his arm at the wrong tempo, but it didn't matter. He quickly found the right key, and Dora played the piano at the right speed no matter what her husband did. Don's joyful countenance and booming baritone lifted spirits throughout the church.

From her vantage point on the platform, Darlene watched her father lead songs and couldn't help but smile. Polly was right—he was cute with his thick blond mustache, twinkly eyes, and contagious smile! Though sometimes he embarrassed her, she honestly adored the man. He didn't anger easily, but the injuries to the van had sorely tried his patience.

After the pastor read a passage from Ephesians, the choir rose. Mrs. McKinley, the choir director, lifted her trembly hands and nodded to Dora for the prelude. Darlene joined her rich contralto voice in harmony, " 'When morning gilds the skies my heart awaking cries, May Jesus Christ be praised.' "

The choir finished and dispersed; Darlene came to the pew

directly in front of Peter and Polly Shackleton to sit beside her
little brother. Her father announced cheerfully, "Before our
next song, turn and greet the people around you. Members, try
to introduce yourselves to one of our visitors."

Darlene turned with outstretched hand. "Hello." She nearly
pulled back when she realized she was greeting a strange
man.

"Enjoyed your song." A firm but gentle clasp warmed her
hand.

"Thank you," she said, looking through his dark-framed
glasses into friendly brown eyes. "Welcome to our church.
I'm Darlene Althorp."

"I know. I'm Jake Edgewood. We met the other night,
remember? Is this your brother?"

Since Darlene was speechless, her brother answered for
himself, shaking the man's hand heartily. "I'm Dustin. That's
our dad up there leading songs. Are you a pilot?" Dustin
guessed, clued by the visitor's acquaintance with Peter
Shackleton.

"No, I'm a Weapons System Officer, or Wizzo, in the Strike
Eagle."

"Far out!" Anything to do with jets fascinated Darlene's
brothers, and the Strike Eagle was their favorite fighter
plane. Dustin would have loved to ply Edgewood with questions, but other people crowded around to meet the visitor.

Still distracted, Darlene shook hands with Polly and Peter.
Polly winked at her. "Yep, Peter knew Jake Edgewood, all
right," she whispered. "Hope you're not sorry I asked! He's
very nice, like you said."

Darlene smiled rather vacantly, then her eyes returned to
Jake. So this was the man about whom she'd been daydreaming impossible romances since Tuesday. He wasn't the
gorgeous heartthrob she'd imagined him into. Standing
beside muscular Peter, he looked almost skinny. He was neither handsome nor homely. His appeal lay in that rare smile

and those warm brown eyes, though shining black hair and a deep tan didn't hurt.

Darlene was distracted during the rest of the service, sensing every move the man behind her made. The pastor must have preached a good sermon, for the visitor said an occasional soft "Amen" and turned to every cross-reference, but Darlene made only a pretense of listening. She smoothed her skirt, brushed back her hair, and shifted position. Was he watching? Did he think she was pretty? Her efforts to attract were more instinctive than calculated.

After the benediction, Dora Althorp played a final chorus on the piano while people made their way to the door, then hurried to collect her Bible and purse from the seat beside her daughter. "Darlene, I'm going to invite the visitor for lunch today, the man who sat behind us. Would you come with me to ask him?"

Darlene wasn't surprised. Her mother always planned a large meal on Sunday, just in case there might be visitors at church. Today a magnificent roast waited in the oven at home; Darlene had prepared it herself.

"Mom, he's the man I hit mirrors with Tuesday night."

Dora brightened. "Is he? Oh, that's wonderful! He called last night and your father invited him to church. It looks like maybe Peter did, too."

"You never told me he called," Darlene protested. "What happened?"

"Oh, they decided we'll each pay for our own damages without involving insurance companies. It wasn't anyone's fault, after all." Dora was more interested in catching up with Edgewood than in giving details.

Overtaking him in the center aisle, she caught him by the sleeve. "I didn't have a chance to greet you earlier and tell you how happy we are to have you here today. I'm Dora Althorp. You spoke with my husband, Don, last night, I hear."

Dora's little hand looked white and soft as she clasped

Jake's sinewy brown hand. "Yes. Pleased to meet you, Mrs. Althorp. Enjoyed your piano playing. I'm Jake Edgewood."

"Do you have plans for the afternoon, Mr. Edgewood, or will you join our family for Sunday dinner? Darlene put a beautiful roast in the oven this morning, plenty for all of us."

"Thank you. Sounds great. I haven't had a home-cooked meal in months."

Darlene thought he gave her a quick glance before accepting, but later she doubted that impression. From the first, Jake made it clear that to him Darlene was merely one of the Althorp children. He invited her and the boys to ride to their house from church with him.

Dustin claimed the front seat. Jake tried to make him relinquish it, but Darlene was just as happy to sit in back with Derrick. Though it was difficult to appear graceful while climbing into a sport/utility vehicle, she did have a good view of Mr. Edgewood's profile from its rear seat. His features were strong: high cheekbones, wide mouth, sharp nose and chin, thick black eyebrows over deep-set eyes. He had a foreign look, but his voice was entirely American.

"So your mother schools you at home, does she?" he was saying. "What grade are you in this year?"

Dustin said, "Fourth."

"Seventh." That was Derrick.

"How about you, Darlene?"

"I should complete my senior year by this fall. I've already applied to a Bible college in the States for the following spring semester." She leaned forward in order to be heard.

"How old are you, if you don't mind me asking?"

"I'll be seventeen in April."

"Sounds like you enjoy school. That's refreshing. I taught high school for a couple years before I entered the air force. Most of my students were unmotivated."

"What subjects did you teach?"

"History, civics, government, and I coached the swim team

and the water polo team. How long have you been home schooled?"

"Mom started teaching us at home four years ago, and I love it."

"What subjects interest you most?"

"History, English lit, and biology. Where did you go to college?"

"I attended a Christian college for two years, then got my degree from Oregon State. Then, like I said, I taught school and worked on a master's degree before attending Officer Training School and getting a commission."

Dustin reclaimed his attention. "Did you always want to be a Wizzo?"

"I had hoped to be a pilot, but my eyesight isn't good enough. God had other plans for me. I enjoy what I do."

"How old are you?"

"Twenty-six. How old are you?"

"I'll be nine in March. Derrick is twelve. Our big sister, Danielle, just got married. She's twenty and lives in Ohio. Do you have any brothers and sisters?"

"I have one big sister, no brothers. You're lucky to have both." Jake followed Don's sedan into a quiet village street and parked in front of the two-story house. Dustin was out of the car before its engine stopped.

"Nice place," Edgewood remarked as they all climbed out.

"It's got a huge garden in back," Derrick told him.

Dustin was already running for the garden gate. "Come see." As soon as the gate opened, a small brown missile burst through and aimed itself at Darlene's legs with ecstatic whimpering cries.

"This is my puppy, François LeBeau. I got him for Christmas. He's six months old." Darlene tried to keep the dog from snagging her nylons. "I love you, too, but get down!"

Edgewood squatted and stretched a hand to the poodle. "Howdy, François."

The pup sniffed his fingers, pom-pom wagging happily.

"He likes you."

"Mr. Edgewood," Dustin commanded, "come see my playhouse."

Edgewood straightened and glanced at Dora, who waved him on. "Go ahead. We'll be a few minutes getting dinner on the table."

"Call me to set the table or chop stuff up. I'm willing to work for my supper."

"All right, I will."

Darlene could hardly believe how relaxed their guest seemed at the dining table. Her parents' openhearted hospitality made some first-time guests ill at ease, but Jake Edgewood thrived under Dora's ministrations. Darlene thought her mother overdid the kindness, offering food until the poor guest could hold no more; Jake only smiled and politely declined to stuff himself. He conversed freely with Don, and the two men discovered many common interests, including tennis. Before the meal ended, they had agreed to test each other's skill on the courts the next Saturday morning.

"Our oldest daughter, Danielle, recently married a seminary student," Dora announced during a conversational lull. "Actually, Blake is already pastoring a church even though he's still in school."

"Dustin told me about them. I hope to meet Danielle and Blake someday, Mrs. Althorp. You have a wonderful family," Edgewood said. "They're an excellent advertisement for the benefits of home schooling."

Dora beamed. "Thank you. We're proud of them. Did you attend public schools?"

"Until seventh grade, then I switched to private school." Edgewood folded his napkin and laid it beside his plate. "That was a great meal, ma'am. Home cooking is a rare treat for me these days. Thank you for letting me join your family today."

"You're more than welcome. There's pie for dessert. Would you like it now or later?"

Edgewood looked to Don for his answer. Mr. Althorp patted his mustache with his napkin. "I don't have room for another bite. Would you care to take a walk with us, Jake?"

"He promised to watch me shoot off model rockets," Dustin interjected. "Can we go now?"

"Why don't we help the ladies clean up the kitchen first? Then we'll all take a stroll together," Don suggested, to the delight of his wife and daughter and the disgust of his sons.

Jake helped clear the table, scraped the plates into the rubbish bin, then surrendered the dishrag to Darlene. Dora handed him a dish towel. "You help Don wipe the dishes, and I'll put them away," she ordered briskly, shooing him out of the way so she could put leftovers into the refrigerator.

"Yes, ma'am." He seemed to enjoy her casual treatment.

She placed her fists on her round hips. "Why don't we make that *Dora?* It makes me feel old to be *ma'amed* by a man."

"Yes, ma'am—I mean Dora." He grinned teasingly.

She zapped at him with a towel, narrowly missing his hip pocket. Darlene watched her mother in amazement and some embarrassment, but Edgewood didn't appear to mind the familiarity.

Dora asked, "Is Jake short for Jacob?"

"No. My initials are *J. K. E.*, therefore, 'Jake.' " His eyes glinted as he pushed up his glasses with one finger. "Almost every fighter pilot or Wizzo has a nickname. It's inescapable."

"What do the *J* and the *K* stand for?" she persisted.

"That's classified." He smiled, but there was a certain set to his jaw.

"He could tell you, but he'd have to shoot you afterwards. That's what he told me when I asked," Dustin piped up.

For a moment Dora was speechless, a condition that could not last. "Utter nonsense! If your mother saw fit to give you two Christian names, I can't believe she would have chosen as badly as that. She raised you too well to be the kind that would give her son a shocking name. What is it? Johannes Kilroy? Jehoshaphat Kristoff?"

Jake shook his head. "Guess all you like. I'll never tell."

Don chuckled. "Don't underestimate the determination of this woman, Jake. She'll pick up that gauntlet and dog you till your dying day."

"I'll take my chances. Now, if my name started with a *D*, I'd be in trouble. Your family has already used up most of the *D* names. Must get confusing sometimes."

Don nodded ruefully. "You ought to hear me stutter when I try to get after one of them. '*Dan-Dar-Der-Dus*—Whoever you are, get over here!' "

⌘

It was unusually warm for February, the perfect afternoon for a walk. The village common was a special plot of undeveloped land with narrow pathways wandering amid ancient English oaks, gorse, and brambles. Local dogs enjoyed chasing rabbits through its grassy fields, and local children made secret hide-outs in its hollows. Even in the dead of winter the common was a pleasant place, providing a "wilderness retreat" only a few minutes' walk from the center of town.

Forgetting to be self-conscious, Darlene ran ahead with the boys and François to find the perfect rocket-launching area. The men maintained a slower pace, discussing the church and sharing spiritual concerns. Dora had opted to remain home and work on a quilt.

The rockets were a great success until a breeze caught one and wafted the parachute beyond a row of houses. Don accompanied Dustin on the search, leaving Derrick, Darlene, and Jake to keep an eye on the launch pad. They found a dry patch and sat down to doze in the thin winter sunshine. Except for the hum of cars on a nearby road and an occasional breeze disturbing the bare branches overhead, perfect silence hung over the common. It didn't take long for Derrick to hop up and declare his intent to explore, leaving the other two alone.

A muffled yelp disturbed the silence. François was nose down in a rabbit burrow. Jake glanced at Darlene. "Think he'll catch a rabbit?"

"I hope not. He's merciless to the mice around our house. He's only a puppy, but he's an excellent hunter—better than some cats." It suddenly occurred to Darlene that she was alone with a young man, and she stiffened. Up until that moment she had felt perfectly relaxed. She studied Jake's profile with cocked head. Perhaps she hadn't felt nervous with him because he was too old to see her as a potential girlfriend, but then, he wasn't all that old. Maybe because he was too short? More likely it was because he did not seem to think of her as a girl at all.

Jake admitted, "Never thought I'd like a poodle, but he's got personality."

"He's my baby! I don't know what he'll do when I go off to college next year."

She whistled, and François came running, his tags jingling. Dirt coated his smooth muzzle and caked his fluffy topknot; gorse and blackberry thorns adorned the poufs on his legs; mud dripped from his lolling pink tongue. "You look disgusting. Trying to dig out the bunnies again, I see," she remarked, brushing at the evidence. He wagged a dirty pompom.

"You've done a great job with him; I've seldom seen a better-behaved dog."

Darlene couldn't hide her pleasure. That tense feeling in her stomach dissolved as she ruffled the pup's ears and made little kissing noises. "I love animals, but Dad says one pet is enough while we live here."

Jake lay back in the grass, pulled off his glasses, and draped one forearm across his eyes. His good clothes were getting soiled, but he didn't seem to care. "What other pet would you have, if you could have any one you chose?"

Darlene's eyes grew dreamy. "I think I'd want a horse. I read about horses a lot, but I've never even sat on one. I like heavy horses best: Shires, Clydesdales, Suffolk Punches."

"Why heavy horses?"

She sighed. "I can imagine Richard the Lionhearted riding one, or Henry the Eighth, or William the Conqueror. Heavy horses are the horses of English history."

"You're a romantic."

"I guess so. I've always dreamed of being loved devotedly by a magnificent horse—you know, like in books. François loves me, but he's only a little poodle."

Jake rolled to his side and propped his head on one hand to look up at her. His eyes looked different without glasses; they were a gorgeous deep brown, with thick black lashes. "Does his small size mean he loves you less?"

She blinked. "Of course not, but it doesn't seem like such a great accomplishment to make a miniature poodle love me as it would be to make a Shire stallion love me."

"Does the source of love determine its value? Or is its value proportionate to the effort expended in acquiring it?"

Darlene struggled to comprehend his rapid questions. "What do you mean?"

"Is François's love less valuable than a horse's love because François is less valuable than a horse? François loves you simply because you are kind to him. Wouldn't a horse be the same?"

She stared, trying to read his meaning in his eyes. Was he serious? "I guess so."

"Or think about this on another level: Nothing is more magnificent and powerful than God, and He loves you more than anyone could. Would His love be more valuable had you worked to earn it?"

Darlene felt outguessed. "That's not the same. How can you compare a horse's love with God's love?"

"It was just a thought. Real love doesn't have to be earned, though perhaps an animal's love does." His smile lighted his face and made him look much younger. "You'll have to get used to my philosophical diversions. Getting back to the subject of horses, why don't you take riding lessons? There are several stables around here."

"Money." She sighed. "I'm saving for college, and Mom and Dad can't spare the extra cash for a nonessential like riding lessons."

"That's too bad." He looked pensive. "I was thinking you could join my Tuesday-evening group class."

"You're taking lessons?"

He nodded. "I'm not great at it, but it's fun. The stable has a Shire mare. I've ridden her a few times. By the way, was your dad upset about the broken mirror? He seemed calm when I called last night."

Darlene took a moment to follow the change in topic. "The mirror? Oh, he was upset, but he didn't blame me for it. He was just. . .upset in general, if you know what I mean."

"Can't blame him for that. It's a pain in the neck to get parts for American cars over here. He was thankful to have you home safe and sound, I'm sure." Jake stood up and brushed off the seat of his tan jeans. "Looks like they found the rocket and parachute."

Darlene stood up and suddenly felt self-conscious again. Jake's trim hips contrasted sharply with her own well-rounded backside, and she felt sure everyone present must be noticing.

"Sorry we took so long. The parachute was caught in a tree, but it was low enough for Dad to reach." Dustin ran ahead of his father to explain.

"You're lucky. It could have ended up in the top of any of these trees," Darlene told him shortly. She was ready to go home, and she didn't want any pie.

three

"Mom!" Darlene's voice nearly rattled the windows. "Derrick used my pencils again, and he left them out and François chewed on them!" Brandishing the gnawed colored pencils, she marched into the kitchen where her mother was washing breakfast dishes. "They're destroyed! I can't take it anymore! Those boys use my things without asking and ruin them all the time!"

Dora turned with a sigh to face her daughter. "Honey, I'm sorry. I'll have a talk with them again about respecting your property, and Derrick will buy you a new set of pencils if he left them out. But please don't say this happens 'all the time.' You know that's an exaggeration."

Derrick burst into the kitchen behind his sister, red-faced with indignation. "I did not use her stupid pencils! She probably left them out herself and now she wants me to buy new ones for her! Mom, she barged into our room without knocking and threw papers all over the floor."

"They were the papers you drew on with my pencils! How dare you say you didn't use them?" Darlene raged.

"I didn't! I used my own pencils! I don't know how yours got out, but I didn't do it. Your stupid dog probably got them out by himself!" Toe-to-toe, Derrick and Darlene shouted, their blue eyes flashing.

"Children," Dora finally got a word in between their accusations. "That is enough!" Her own eyes shot sparks. "Not another word, or your father will be hearing about this! Both of you, go to your rooms and stay there until I come to talk with you. Shame on you for behaving this way! You sound like a pair of wildcats!"

Fuming silently, the pair exited together, casting bitter

24

glares at one another all the way up the stairs. Back in the kitchen, Dora rubbed a shaking hand across her forehead and sighed deeply. She already had a headache, and this battle, the latest of many, was not making her feel any better.

There was a knock at the front door. François barked all the way downstairs, jarring on each step: "Woo-woo-woo-woof!" He skidded to the door, nearly bashing his pointed nose.

"Hush, now," Dora warned him, pushing him away from the door with her foot while she opened it.

François evaded her foot and stuck his head outside, ready to defend his home to the death. His pom-pom began to wiggle, then wag furiously, and he let out a happy cry of welcome.

"Hello, Dora." Jake pulled off his flight cap.

"Jake!" Dora tried to sound pleased to see him, though his timing was not the best. "What brings you here?"

"I promised Don this book the other day, and thought I'd drop it by on my way to work." He paused, then asked, "Are you all right?"

Dora wondered if he'd heard the battle raging from outside. "I'll survive. We're having sibling warfare today. Darlene and Derrick, this time."

He looked sincerely troubled. "You look tired out."

Dora smiled wistfully. "I am, and it's not yet noon. I've got a splitting headache, and I just don't know what to do with these children sometimes. We discipline them diligently, talk to them till we're blue in the face, read Scripture to them, and have Bible studies on peace and unselfish love, but it doesn't seem to sink in."

Jake checked his watch. "I have a few minutes to spare. I'd be happy to pray with you before you talk with them. Would that help?"

Dora started to turn his offer down, then reconsidered. "Why not? Yes, it will help, I'm sure!"

She led him to the living room where he sat beside her on the sofa, rested his elbows on his knees, and bowed his head.

Twisting her hands together, Dora tried to begin, but almost immediately choked up. Jake quietly prayed for her, "Lord, You know the pain Dora is suffering, both physical and emotional. Please ease her pain; help her to see her children objectively, the way You see them, and give her wise words of counsel. I thank You for the examples of unselfish love that Don and Dora are, and I ask that You would transmit their maturity and wisdom to their children."

Dora had recovered enough to speak. "Yes, Lord, I thank You for Your promise that You will supply the wisdom I need; I only have to ask for it. Lord, You know my heartache for Darlene—she says she loves You, but her love for You is so shallow! Please make Yourself real to her; help her to know You as her dearest Friend and Lover. And Lord, please help Derrick to be more thoughtful of his brother and sister, and to try not to antagonize them. I know he loves You, but he is still very much a child. Please give me wisdom as their mother to guide them firmly and lovingly in Your paths." Once she got started, Dora poured out a flood of requests for her husband and children.

When she finished, Jake rose to fetch her a box of tissues and sat patiently waiting while she wiped her face and blew her nose. "Better?"

She nodded, "Yes, thank you."

"You're quite a mother to take on schooling your children this way."

She sighed. "Not really. I enjoy it most of the time. I dearly love our children and enjoy spending time with them, but their human natures frustrate me no end! They look for faults in one another and try to find ways to get one another into trouble! Why are they like that, Jake? We work so hard to teach them Christlike love and maturity, and they fight it tooth and nail!"

"You've already identified the problem, Dora—their human natures. They really are good kids, but there's room for improvement in all of us, and I'm sure you and Don want only the best from your children."

"Maybe we expect too much—"

"I didn't say that. I don't think you can expect too much; they need a high goal to strive for. After all, as it says in Philippians three, chapter fourteen, our prize is 'the high calling of God in Christ Jesus.' Nothing you and Don demand from them can be higher than that goal."

Dora sat up and straightened her plump shoulders. "You're right, Jake. I can't tell you how much I appreciate this—you're exactly what I needed this morning: a breath of fresh air. I wish you could stay and teach our history lesson!"

He smiled his gentle smile. "I wish I could, too, but I'm flying today, an upgrade ride." He rose and pulled his flight cap from his ankle pocket. "Tell the kids 'hello' for me."

Dora followed him to the front door. "Do you have a girlfriend, Joseph Kirk?"

He gave her a curious look. "Sort of. Why?" Her not-so-subtle attempt to guess his name amused him.

"I just wondered. There aren't many young men like you around these days—men who would offer to pray with an overwrought mother, that is."

"Are you matchmaking, Dora?" His eyes twinkled as he squatted to pet François.

"Well, the thought did enter my mind. . .what do you mean by 'sort of'?"

"There's a girl back home. . .I've thought about marrying her. There's nothing definite between us, though. We're good friends. We've discussed going into foreign missions together someday, but it's just talk."

"What's her name?"

"Teri Sutton. Her brother, Reg, is married to my adopted sister, Leigh."

"Adopted sister?" Dora couldn't help digging for more information.

"Yes. I was adopted by the Edgewood family when I was twelve."

"Oh." Surprise made Dora pause.

"Anything else you want to know?" He wasn't smiling, but he didn't seem angry, so she ventured one more question.

"Is she pretty?"

"Teri?" He looked startled by the question. "I never really thought about it. She's no beauty, but she has a heart for the Lord and a real love for people." He studied Dora's revealing face for a moment. "Darlene is too young for me, Dora. I'm ten years older than she is."

"I know. I was thinking ahead. She'll be seventeen in a few weeks, and eighteen only a year after that! I just wish God would send a man like you for her. Danielle has a dear husband, but then she's such a cute, sweet little thing—she could take her choice of men. Darlene, well, she has a hot temper and she's built like her father and. . .I worry about her sometimes, Jake."

"I wouldn't. She has potential, and she'll grow into it, given time. With a mother like you, how can she miss?" He touched his cap and headed for his car. "See you later."

"Bye, Jephthah Keith." Dora watched him drive away before heading upstairs to discipline her children. Her headache had vanished.

❧

"This is Monte; he's mine. Dustin's is named Reba; he wants her to have babies. We could sell them easily at the pet shop."

"I thought your dad would allow only one pet in the family," Jake said, regarding Derrick's pet dubiously.

Derrick placed the brown and white rat on Jake's shoulder. "Who told you that? He let each of us get one pet. Dustin and I got these for Christmas, but Mom says they have to live in the garage."

Giving a meaningful sniff, Jake said, "Can't imagine why." The rat stood on its hind legs and sniffed at his ear, making him wince.

"Yeah, I guess it doesn't smell too good out here," Derrick admitted. "Don't his whiskers tickle?"

"Yes." The word came out rather forcefully. "Does it bite?"

"He bit me once, but that was a long time ago. I think he likes you, Jake."

"I'm honored."

Derrick missed the sarcasm or ignored it.

Dustin entered the tiny garage, panting from his hurry. "Hey, you didn't tell me you were coming out here! I want to show Jake my Reba." He opened the cage, lifted his rat out, and murmured endearments to it, nose to nose. "Wanna hold her, Jake? She's really sweet." Without waiting for a response, he plopped his rat on Jake's other shoulder.

"Stop it, Dustin. What if they fight?" Derrick's changing voice cracked slightly.

Jake looked alarmed. "Are they likely to?" Reba examined his other ear, then tried to climb down his chest head first.

"They might. They're not used to each other."

"Wonderful. Please remove them from my person," Jake requested.

Too late. Reba discovered a gap between two of his shirt buttons and slipped inside his flannel shirt before Dustin could grab her.

"Ahhgh!" Jake backed up, bending forward at the waist and holding the shirt away from his body.

The other rat started climbing down his back, sliding to his belt. By this time the two boys were laughing uncontrollably. Only fear for his pet's safety prompted Derrick to remove Monte before he could slip beneath Jake's belt and cause worse havoc.

Jake hurriedly untucked his shirt and tried to grab the female rat, but she eluded his grasp and made her way to the back of his shirt between his shoulder blades. Jake gave up and held still. "Dustin, get your rat off my back, please." He had to suppress a grin in spite of himself. The boys' amusement was contagious, and he knew he must look funny.

"What are you doing out here? We could hear you from the house," Darlene asked from the doorway. "Jake, are you all right?" She shut her dog outside. François whined and scratched at the closed door.

"Aside from the fact that I have a rat on my back, I'm fine." He stood bent over, shoulder blades back, his arms at a ridiculous angle, wincing every time the rat made a move.

"Under your shirt?" Darlene asked, moving closer for a better look. Then she, too, burst into giggles. "You look so funny!"

"I'm sure I do, but please help me. I've got an awful feeling it's not housebroken."

"That doesn't matter; we're not in the house." Darlene tried to look serious, but couldn't hold a straight face. "Wish I had a camera."

"Darlene!" His voice rose.

"Oh, all right." She moved toward him, then felt her face grow hot. The thought of reaching up his shirt to find the rat made her knees feel rubbery. "Dustin, come get your rat."

"You get her," Dustin rebelled, loath to take an order from his sister.

"Dustin!" Jake's good nature had reached its limit.

Dustin recovered his rat. Reba left her hiding place reluctantly, leaving faint scratch marks down Jake's back. "Ouch!" he protested, then groped with one hand to feel for damage.

"I think you'll live," Darlene teased. It was a novelty to see Jake's composure ruffled.

"Thanks, doc." He straightened to watch Dustin put the rat away. "Great pets, guys, but I like them better in their cages. Actually, I don't do well with rodents."

"Neither does François. If he ever got ahold of those two, they wouldn't stand a chance."

"Good for François."

"Aw, man!" the boys protested.

He held up one hand. "Sorry, but that's how I feel. My vote's for the poodle. Hey, while I've got the three of you alone, there's something I've wanted to say."

"Uh-oh," Derrick blurted. "Sounds like a lecture."

"You're right, but listen anyhow."

"Fire away," Darlene prompted when he paused.

"I think you've got the greatest family in the world, and it burns me up to hear the way you three snipe at each other. Don't you know how it hurts your mother, not to mention how you hurt each other when you fight? I grew up wishing I had a home like yours, and it galls me to see how little you appreciate what you've got."

Derrick's head drooped. Jake had never berated them before. Shame washed over each of them at his words.

"Worst of all was the day when I heard you fighting all the way from the street. What was that fight about? Oh yeah, colored pencils. I could hardly believe that one. I found your mom in tears. We prayed together for each of you. Did she tell you?"

Darlene shook her head. Her eyes burned. He had heard her! Screaming like a wildcat, her mother had said, and she knew it was true. Jake was the last person she would want to hear her screams of rage.

"I haven't got any more to say except: Please try to get along better, to be kinder to one another, for your parents' sake and for the Lord's. You can't have much of a testimony for Him with that kind of noise coming from your house. Try reading Ephesians chapter four, and memorize verse thirty-two."

Unable to meet his eyes or reply, Darlene hurried back to the house while her tears spilled over.

She did memorize that verse. So did the boys. It helped.

four

"Telephone's ringing," Darlene caroled, hurrying to answer it. She had just finished recopying her final draft of a term paper and felt on top of the world. "I'll get it!"

"Hello?" Her melodious voice held a lilt.

"Darlene? This is Jake."

"Jake! Hello! Are you home from Turkey?"

"Not yet. I'm calling from my room at Inçirlik."

"Oh! You sound so close. I didn't know you had telephones in your rooms."

"We do now. They've upgraded the living quarters here, and I can call out using my calling card."

"Do you want to talk to Dad or Mom?"

"Don't you want to talk to me?" He sounded hurt, oddly enough. "I'd like to hear how you've been spending your time while I've been away all spring."

"School, girls' club activities, and some baby-sitting. I'm also working as a bagger at the base commissary sometimes. I've earned nearly enough to pay my half of college tuition for next year!" She was pleased with herself and not ashamed to admit it.

"Good girl! How are your classes going? You've started your senior year work now, right?"

"Yes, I just finished writing my last term paper for eleventh grade, so now I'm officially in twelfth. Did you ever take calculus? I think it's going to be the death of me!"

He chuckled. "Yeah, I died from the same cause a few years back. You'll make it, Little Miss Brain. I'll give you some coaching when I get back if you really think you need it. Math wasn't my best subject, but I'll see what I can do to help."

Little! Darlene suddenly felt dainty and feminine. It was a wonderful feeling. "Thanks, Jake." Her heart pounded in the strangest way. "When will you be home?"

"In just over a week. I'm ready to head out now, but no can do. This place gets deadly boring after a few weeks, and it's hotter than the fiery furnace during the summer. Say, I've got a surprise for you when I get back—sort of a late birthday present. Your parents know all about it."

"They do? What is it?"

"You'll find out. Got to keep it a surprise."

To his surprise, Darlene didn't beg, but asked, "What have you been doing? Are you flying much?"

"Almost every day. Not much is going on, but I suppose that's good news. We had to come back early yesterday; had a computer malfunction. Nothing serious, but enough to bring us back to base."

"Who is your pilot?"

"I've been crewed with a couple different guys. Pete Shackleton was here, and I flew with him for a while, but he's gone back home. I suppose you've seen him at church."

"Yes, I have."

"Now I'm crewed with a guy named Bill Frembling, or 'Otter.' He's a good guy, though a bit heavy-handed on the stick."

"Oh," Darlene nodded as though she knew what he was talking about. "I guess you must have heard that Polly Shackleton is expecting."

"No, I hadn't heard! Hey, that's great!"

"Yeah. She passed out at the Mildenhall Air Show; that was their first clue that something might be different." Darlene chuckled. "She hasn't been feeling well lately."

"Hope she doesn't get too sick. Say, I hate to cut this short, but I'd better go. It's been good talking with you."

"Oh, yes! Thank you for calling, Jake. I'll see you soon."

"God bless you, Darlene. I've been praying for you."

"You have?" She felt breathless. "Why?"

"You've been on my mind a lot, I guess. Give your family my love."

Darlene stared at the telephone for a long time after hanging up. "He's been praying for me?" she murmured, feeling her heart give a flip-flop. Why a simple thing like prayer would have that effect, she wasn't sure. "He called all the way from Turkey and only talked to me!" Now that fact was worthy of a few palpitations!

During the months since their February crash-meeting, Jake had become part of the Althorp family. He played tennis with Don and usually won, played golf with Don and usually lost. The two men also worked together on an outreach team and had started a men's prayer meeting which met early Friday mornings. When he was on a late flying schedule, Jake often came to the Althorp house in the mornings and helped Dora teach history and civics classes. He made woodworking projects with the boys, taught them to design and build kites, and helped them create realistic Civil War battle scenes using their tiny metal figurines. Sunday lunch was an established tradition; Jake always came home with the family after church.

Darlene often felt somewhat left out, for Jake did not teach her classes or do projects with her, although he occasionally read her term papers and made suggestions for improvement. Since the day with the rats, she always had to seek out his attention, ask for his advice, and request his opinion. He gave of these freely when she asked, but he never offered them of his own accord again. Frustrated, Darlene had taken time from her studies to learn how to make a birdhouse with her brothers, although woodcrafting had never interested her in the past. She had even, to her father's amazement, joined in games of tag football with the boys and men just to be a part of the action.

Darlene had learned to treasure Jake's rare compliments. He seldom said a word about her appearance, her lovely singing voice, her sewing skills, or her exceptional cooking abilities, but he occasionally mentioned a character trait that he admired, such as her willingness to help her mother, the way she looked for opportunities to serve her father, or the time she defended Dustin when Derrick ridiculed one of his art projects.

It had been months since the last time she and Derrick quarreled. They still occasionally butted heads, but they were learning to work out their disagreements in constructive ways.

"Does he know how much I've changed?" she wondered aloud.

୬

Upon his return from Turkey, Jake slipped easily into his old routine, spending most of his free time at the Althorp home. He didn't immediately reveal his "surprise" to Darlene; he made her wait a few days. Then, one Tuesday afternoon, he stopped by the house after work.

Darlene met him at the door. "Howdy, Jake! What's up?" Her long blond hair was in two pigtails, and, except for her womanly figure, she looked like a very tall little girl in pink shorts and a flowery top.

"Just checking to make sure you're home. Tonight is your surprise."

Her face lit up. "It is? What's happening?"

"Just be ready by six-thirty. Wear long pants and shoes with a low heel, like hiking boots."

Darlene stepped out onto the porch. She was barefooted, and Jake's heavy flight boots gave him extra height, making him slightly taller for the moment. She liked looking up at him. "I'll be ready. Are we going for a hike?" That didn't sound terribly exciting, but the chance to be with him would be fun no matter where they went.

He smiled, and his dark eyes twinkled. He did have the cutest smile!

"No, we're not going for a hike. I can't believe you haven't guessed yet. I'll be back to pick you up, kiddo. Don't keep me waiting."

Darlene watched him walk back to his car, admiring how square his shoulders and how trim his hips looked in that flight suit. His attractions were definitely growing on her.

☙

It was such a thrill to bid her family good-bye and climb into the front seat of Jake's Cherokee! She could imagine, with very little effort, that they were going on a date. Jake's manner was far from romantic, however, which was probably just as well. She could never have had so much fun with a man who acted romantic and mushy; she would have been far too self-conscious to enjoy herself.

Settling back for a long drive, she could hardly believe her eyes when he turned into a back road not far from her house. "Where are we going?"

"You'll see."

Minutes later he turned into the drive of a riding stable, and Darlene flung herself at him in happy abandon, clutching his arm with both hands. "We're going horseback riding? Oh, Jake! I can't believe it! I never knew this stable was here!"

"This is where I take lessons every week—or I do when I'm in the country," he amended. "I signed you up for a lesson this week, my treat."

The sight, scent, and sound of horses filled Darlene's senses when he opened her door for her. The stable was old and slightly run down, but beautiful faces peered over the half-door of each stall. Perhaps the buildings suffered from neglect, but the horses did not.

Jake introduced her to their instructor and showed her where to select a safety helmet. Then he bid her good-bye with a squeeze of her shoulder and a comradely wink. Darlene was the only first-time student that evening, so she had her own private introductory class while the other students brought out and mounted their horses.

Libby, her teacher, quickly went over the basics she would be required to know before mounting her horse, and Darlene concentrated hard. "Jake tells me you wish to ride a Shire horse. Is that right?"

Darlene nodded. "If it's convenient. I've never ridden any horse at all."

"Wilhelmina is one of our gentlest horses, so she'll be ideal for you to begin on." Libby led the way down a row of stalls while she spoke. "She is already saddled and bridled for you. If you take further lessons, you'll eventually be required to saddle and bridle your own mount, but for now we do that for you."

No face appeared over the stall door where they stopped. Darlene peered into the darkness within and was startled to see an enormous rump facing her. "Come, Willa my love, and meet Darlene," Libby cooed, unlatching the door. With a low nicker, the massive animal turned to face them. Thrusting her head over the door, she reached her pink nose toward Darlene.

"Hello, Wilhelmina," Darlene murmured hesitantly. That great Roman nose, the heavily muscled neck, and those gentle brown eyes were everything she had dreamed of, but the reality of her dream was more daunting than she had expected.

Libby entered the stall and led the mare out, then handed the reins to Darlene, showing her how to hold them. "Just walk at her shoulder, holding her head far enough away so she won't walk on your heels. Believe me, it hurts when Willa walks on you."

Darlene could well believe it. The mare had hooves the size of dinner plates surrounded by shaggy white "feathers." It was fun to hear them clop on the concrete beside her as she led the horse toward the riding arena. Willa never tried to forge ahead or lag behind. She eyed Darlene curiously, then shook her huge head with a great clatter and rattle of bits and leather. Darlene lost hold of the reins beneath Willa's chin.

"Don't let go of her," Libby warned. "Willa is unlikely to run off on you, but other horses might. Never take chances."

When they reached the arena, Libby went through a long

spiel of instruction about parts of the bridle and saddle, parts of the horse, and how to mount properly. After what seemed an age to Darlene, she was finally allowed to mount Willa. Even with a mounting block it wasn't easy, the horse was so big. She stood patiently for Darlene, however, only munching on her bit.

Darlene tried to listen to Libby, but she couldn't help watching the rest of the class circle the other instructor far out in the arena. It was easy to pick out Jake. He wasn't the only man in the class, but Darlene would have known his slim figure anywhere. He rode well, she could tell—the best in the class.

At last she was allowed to urge Willa into a slow walk. It was delightful to feel that great body beneath hers and sense the horse's response to her commands through the reins or with her legs. The lesson ended far too quickly.

Libby allowed Darlene to unsaddle and unbridle Willa, which was not the usual procedure for a first-time student, but she couldn't resist Darlene's eagerness to help and learn. "Hope you can come back sometime," she said while they carried Willa's tack to the storage room. "You seem to really enjoy horses, and I think Willa liked you."

"Do you?" Darlene glowed. "I liked her, too."

"She isn't the most exciting horse to ride, but she's a good-hearted old thing," Libby admitted. "Maybe you could come work for us to earn another lesson. People do that sometimes."

The idea took hold in Darlene's mind. She could talk of nothing else for days afterward, and her family began to regret ever allowing Jake to take her riding. He, on the other hand, enjoyed her enthusiasm.

"Riding is good exercise for her, and I know you've had trouble finding a physical exercise she enjoys," he argued in Darlene's defense one evening while watching Dora sew pajamas for Dustin. "Working around the stable would be great exercise, believe me."

"But she knows next to nothing about horses, and I'm

afraid she'll be terribly disappointed when it all comes to nothing. We can never afford to buy her a horse, and lessons are dreadfully dear."

"She'll appreciate lessons more if she has to work for them," Jake maintained. "I'll be willing to drive her over there to work a few days, or she could walk. It isn't far."

"But it will take so much of her time," Dora continued, rising to iron a seam. "What we really need is a sport all three children can participate in and enjoy that doesn't cost much. We had discussed swimming, but lessons are expensive, and Darlene would feel silly among a bunch of little children."

Jake was silent for a moment, then mentioned, "I could teach them swimming, if you really want them to learn."

Don stopped reading his magazine to contribute, "That's right; you used to be a swim team coach, didn't you?"

"Yes. I'm a certified instructor, and I'd be willing to teach them, maybe once a week for an hour or two. You'd have to pay for use of the pool, but I'd teach for free—with one condition."

"Which is?" Dora prodded, suspicious.

"That Darlene be allowed to work at the stable occasionally and maybe take a riding lesson once in a while."

"Why does her riding mean so much to you?" Don asked curiously.

He shrugged. "Because it means so much to her. If you had seen the look on her face while she sat on that horse. . ." his voice trailed off. "I like to see her happy."

The knowing little smile on Dora's face sent hot blood into Jake's brown cheeks. "Dora, don't start on me again."

"I didn't say a word!" She chuckled. "Well, what do you think, Don?"

"I think it's worth a try. Don't know how Darlene will feel about it, though. She has never enjoyed swimming. We might have a battle on our hands."

"We might be thankful to have the inducement of riding

lessons, when it comes to that," Dora admitted. "Would you mind teaching one other student? Darlene might feel better about it if there were another girl in the class."

"Who'd you have in mind?"

"Joanna Whitehead. Her parents are always looking for a P.E. program for her, too. You know who she is?"

"Darlene's friend from church. No, I don't mind teaching her too, if you think it will help."

❧

"Mom, you can't be serious!" Darlene protested, dropping her fork with a clatter on her empty salad plate.

"Swimming lessons from Jake? Cool!" Dustin and Derrick enthused.

"Yes, I am quite serious. Your father and I have discussed this at length, and we've decided this is too good an opportunity to pass up. The Whiteheads have agreed to let Joanna take lessons along with you, so you won't be the only girl involved," Dora said firmly.

Darlene huffed and rolled her eyes. "And I don't have any say in this at all? Dad, I'm seventeen years old!" She appealed to a higher authority.

Don Althorp nodded thoughtfully as he took another helping of spaghetti. "Yup. High time you had swimming lessons. Too bad we didn't have this chance years ago."

His daughter spotted the teasing glint in his blue eyes, but she was not amused. "I don't want to take swimming lessons. How embarrassing! I don't even have a bathing suit. Let him teach the boys, but leave me out of this."

Dora's lips formed a determined line. "Darlene, you must realize that the greatest weakness in our home-school program has been the lack of physical education. Derrick loves any sport, but you and Dustin—"

Darlene tried to interrupt, but her mother lifted a restraining hand. "No, listen to me. We have tried tennis, gymnastics, golf, running on the base track, and who knows how many other things, but you've managed to squirm your way out of every last one. You're becoming a couch potato, my dear, and Dustin is following your example."

Darlene slumped in her chair, eyes smoldering, and Dustin punched Derrick, who had made a mocking face.

"Boys! Enough! Derrick, that was entirely uncalled for, and Dustin, keep your hands and feet to yourself." Dora's firm voice brought quick results, though the children's facial expressions still indicated rebellion.

Don finished eating and joined the conversation again, addressing Darlene. "We're not trying to be cruel, darlin'. Another year or so and you'll be on your own, making your own decisions about whether or not you exercise your body, but for now your mother and I still make the decisions, and we have decided that swimming lessons will be ideal for you."

Darlene adored her father, but not even he could make this palatable. "But, Dad. . .Jake?"

"He is a certified swimming instructor with plenty of teaching experience, and he has offered to do this for us for free. Swimming is great exercise and is a sport you can all three do together, saving your mother some driving trips. Now, we wouldn't trust just any man to teach you kids, but Jake, as you well know, is above reproach."

Darlene couldn't argue that point. "When are we supposed to start?" She might be able to drop a few pounds first. The worst part of this entire plan was the thought of squeezing her body into a swimsuit.

"Right away. We need to find suitable swimwear for all three of you, so I thought we'd drive over to the BX tonight. We might have to mail order suits, but I'm hoping not. Now, one more thing. If you behave well and work hard at your swimming, your father and I have agreed that you may have one horseback riding lesson a month, and you may occasionally work at the stable to earn extra lessons if you want."

"Really?" Darlene looked to her father, who nodded, smiling, and she clasped her hands in delight. "Thank you! Oh, thank you so much!" This did make the swimming lessons more bearable, but still. . .

Darlene fell silent, and the boys took up her slack, asking countless eager questions. She began to clear the table, listening to their chatter with only half an ear. Once the sink was full of sudsy water and Darlene stayed in one place to wash up, François appeared from under the table and plopped on top of her feet. Darlene wiggled her toes beneath him, smiling fondly, but soon forgot his presence.

Washing dishes was a great time for daydreaming. . .or brooding. Absently scrubbing an already well-scoured pan, she thought about riding Wilhelmina again. She could picture that big head, the broad white blaze and soft, wrinkly pink lips.

"But swimming? I have to wear a bathing suit in front of Jake," she groaned. François readjusted his head on her slippers and wagged his pom-pom. "He'll know exactly how fat I am. What a nightmare!" The idea nearly brought tears.

Dora started through the kitchen with a load of freshly dried laundry. "What's a nightmare, dear?"

Heat crept into Darlene's fair cheeks. "Oh, nothing."

The laundry basket thumped on the tabletop. Dora's curiosity had been aroused. "Are you thinking about swimming still?"

Cheeks growing hotter, Darlene mumbled, "Yes."

Preparing for a good chat, Dora plopped into a chair. "I know Jake isn't your first choice for an instructor, but I don't think it will be as bad as all that. Don't forget about his girlfriend back in the States."

"Mom!" Darlene protested. "I don't suspect him of designs on me. For goodness' sake, he's the last man I'd worry about in that way! He barely knows I'm alive, or at best he thinks I'm a big, fat, goofy girl."

Dora's lips twitched. "Is that so?"

"You know it is." Those dratted tears threatened again.

Dora watched her daughter work for a moment. "I know nothing of the sort. You are tall, yes, but you are neither fat nor goofy. You could have a lovely figure if you worked at it, Darlene, and Jake knows very well how intelligent you are."

Darlene made no reply, so she continued, "I asked Jake about Teri the other day—you know, his alleged girlfriend. I've been wondering why he hasn't married her already. She's working on her master's degree, he said."

"You think he's really in love with her? Somehow I can't imagine Jake being in love," Darlene's humorless chuckle brought a startled glance from her mother. "He isn't the type."

"I wasn't aware that love was limited to any certain 'type' of man. Jake is one of the most loving men I've ever known. I can't believe you're that imperceptive, Darlene."

"Mom, I'm not cutting him down. I know Jake is loving; he's—he's a sweetie, really. He's kind and considerate, full of God's love, and cares about people more than anyone else I know, except maybe you and Dad. It's romantic love I'm talking about. I can't imagine him having heart palpitations over any woman—he's just not like that!"

Dora lifted one eyebrow, her lips pursed. "You don't know men very well if you think Jake is incapable of romance."

Darlene frowned. "Mom, he's not in love with you, is he?"

She was relieved to see her mother dissolve into laughter.

"Oh! Oh, my dear," Dora gasped. "I am highly flattered that you even thought of such a thing, but—" she burst into giggles again.

"Well," Darlene defended herself, "he does spend lots of time with you. He spends most of his free time here at our house."

Dora picked up her clothes basket, her amusement reduced to an occasional chuckle. "Yes, he enjoys our family. He is a lonely young man who craves a loving home and Christian fellowship. That's why he spends hours with me and your father. He enjoys playing with the boys because he's still a boy at heart, and he enjoys you because you're a lovely girl and he is a man. Now be ready to go in ten minutes, all right? We'll need time to pick out swimsuits, and the BX closes awfully early."

"All right," Darlene said as Dora left the room. Placing a clean pan into the rinse water, she considered her mother's words with knitted brows and shook her head. In light of Jake's decidedly unromantic manner, she discounted the idea that he found her attractive.

Once the swimsuits, bathing cap, and towels had been purchased, Darlene felt doomed to swimming lessons. There would be no escape this time unless she could develop some allergy or physical condition. . .not much hope of that. She was disgustingly healthy.

The first swimming lesson was slated for a Saturday morning. Darlene could not sleep the night before, her mind consumed by dread of the morrow. Not even Joanna had sympathized with her, but then Joanna wasn't a very sympathetic person. From the first, she had delighted in teasing Darlene about Jake, assuming that she must have a crush on him.

A crush on Jake? Not that she would ever admit!

"Why does he affect me this way?" she wondered aloud, folding her hands behind her head on the pillow. Although he wasn't particularly handsome, there was something about him. . .but apparently no one else could see this special something. Only last weekend Darlene had spent the night at Joanna's house, and they had argued about Jake.

Darlene couldn't remember exactly how the subject came up, but she vividly recalled Joanna's snort, "Give me a break! Jake is geeky and skinny, Darlene, and I've never heard him laugh. He's like a dried-up old professor with those nerdy glasses. He's too short for you, and my dad says he looks like an Arab or an Indian, he's so brown."

"Who cares what nationality he is? He's a nice man, and he does laugh sometimes," Darlene had maintained, unable to deny that Jake was not a thrill a minute to be around. "He's about a half inch taller than I am, so he's not too short. His eyes are gorgeous when he takes his glasses off. Besides, he really listens when you talk to him, like what you have to say is important. Most grown-ups think you don't have a brain until you've graduated from high school. My dad says Jake is a man after God's own heart, and they're not easy to come by these days."

"Whatever. I still think you could pick someone more interesting to have a crush on."

"I do not have a crush on him!" Darlene had maintained, but Joanna could not be hoodwinked.

Joanna was right; there were other men in the world, ". . .though not many as nice as Jake," Darlene sighed aloud.

François rose from his nest at her feet and tried to join her on the pillow, thinking she wanted his attention. "Lie down, Beau. I wasn't talking to you."

But a moment later she sat up and asked desperately, "François, what am I going to do?"

five

"You go first."

"No, you go first."

Darlene and Joanna tried to hide behind each other when they stepped out of the dressing room swathed in terry cloth cover-ups. Their whispered pleas were hidden beneath the echoing calls of swimmers already in the pool. The humid atmosphere around the enclosed pool reeked of chlorine.

The girls wore yellow caps and matching blue and yellow suits, designed for serious swimming. The high necklines and modestly cut legs were of some comfort, but Darlene was well aware that every bulge was revealed to the world by that uncompromising fabric. Joanna fared no better. The two girls took secret comfort in each other's chubby thighs, but assured each other, "You look great. I'm the fat one."

The boys waited on the bleachers beside the pool, towels draped around their necks. Darlene noticed how blindingly white their skin was and realized that she must look the same. Due to their Nordic heritage, she supposed. Joanna might deplore her freckles, but at least they gave her some color.

"Where's Jake?" Joanna asked, tucking fuzzy brown hair into her swim cap. Darlene's brothers scooted over to make room on the bench.

"Talking to one of the lifeguards."

Darlene spotted him across the pool, talking with another man. Both men were clad in trunks and tank tops, their arms crossed over their chests.

Joanna elbowed her in the side, her gray eyes incredulous. "Wouldja take a look at the professor!"

46

Darlene was already looking. The pool lifeguard's shoulders bulged with muscle, but his midsection also bulged. In contrast, Jake carried not an extra ounce on his bronze body; his arms, chest, and legs looked like sculpture, each muscle clearly defined.

The girls simultaneously realized that Jake was not the wimpy professor Joanna had labeled him. Darlene recalled the few times she had grabbed his arm and felt hard muscle, and she now recognized his easy grace as the movement of a trained athlete. He had often worn shorts and short-sleeved shirts in her presence, but she had never before noticed that his limbs were not skinny, but lean and sinewy.

"Mmmm," Joanna gave her a provocative wink. "Maybe we have something here after all. He looks like a model of 'the Noble Savage.'"

Dustin tugged at Darlene's towel. "I got a secret."

She looked down into her brother's mischievous smile, thankful to escape Joanna's teasing. "What is it? Whose secret?"

"Jake's. When he was putting his stuff in a locker, a letter dropped on the floor, and I found it. It was addressed to Lieutenant Josiah K. Edgewood."

Darlene's eyes widened. "Josiah." She gripped Dustin's arm. "Does he know that you know?"

"Yup. He gave me a funny look when I gave him his letter, but didn't say anything. Here he comes now!" Dustin sat up straight and grinned when Jake caught his eye.

"Sorry I kept you waiting. Wanted to make sure of the pool rules before we started. Ready?" He looked them over quickly, barely skimming the girls with his eyes. "Isn't your mother coming today?"

"She'll be here in a while. She needed to run some errands first."

Dustin gave a knowing little chuckle. Jake grinned sheepishly and ruffled the boy's hair. "You told, didn't you?"

"Told what?" Derrick was quick to ask. "What does he know?"

"I only told Darlene," Dustin admitted.

"What's the big secret?" Joanna demanded. "Tell me too." She batted her big eyes at Jake. Darlene wanted to hit her.

"May I?" Dustin inquired, now that it was too late.

Jake shrugged. "If you must. The damage is done."

"His name is Josiah. I don't see why you wouldn't tell. It's a lot better than the names Mom calls you."

Joanna looked rather shocked, so Darlene explained her mother's habit of calling Jake every combination of names starting with his initials, ". . . like Jehoiachin Konrad and Jerubbabel Kilroy. We won't tell Mom if you don't want us to," she assured Jake. "We still don't know your middle name, anyway."

"It's Kyle. She'll probably guess eventually. There aren't that many names starting with *J,* and if she keeps going through the Old Testament kings she'll hit it eventually." He shrugged his shoulders, looking across the pool as though eager to complete the discussion and get down to business.

"I think Josiah is a nice name," Darlene assured him. "I wish you would let us call you by it."

He only gave her a fleeting glance and smile before announcing, "Let's get started here. Everybody, in the pool and show me what you know."

It turned out to be a surprisingly fun lesson. Jake started with the basics, having them hold their breath underwater while he counted aloud, then demonstrate their ability to kick, tread water, and freestyle swim. Darlene was more advanced than the others, but she was far from proficient and tired quickly. Joanna produced an impressive dog paddle, but refused to open her eyes underwater, claiming that the chlorine hurt them. Derrick thrashed determinedly, but made little forward progress, choking and spluttering when he swallowed water. Dustin released his grip on the wall long enough to dog paddle for thirty seconds, his thin neck straining to keep his chin from touching the surface.

"Good effort," Jake praised, still standing on the side. "You all have a lot to learn, but you show a willing attitude, and that's half the battle. Today we'll concentrate on holding your breath underwater then take time to play and get comfortable in the water."

He coached them through several rounds of breath holding, pleased when Dustin finally immersed his entire face. The boy showed signs of relaxing and of wanting to keep up with his big brother. Joanna and Darlene found this stage of the lessons undemanding and amused themselves by watching other swimmers.

"Look at that man over there," Darlene said with admiration in her voice. "Do you think we'll ever be able to swim like that?"

Jake overheard. "Sure you will. He's doing the butterfly stroke. I'll teach it to you eventually."

"You can do that?" Gripping the side at his feet, Darlene looked up at him. He only nodded, sliding his eyes away from her.

"Come in the water and show us," Derrick demanded, still panting from his exertions. "We're doing all the work."

"As it should be. I'm expending my sadistic proclivities by extracting involuntary labor from the masses," Jake explained.

"Huh?" Dustin inquired, his eyes blank.

"Please? We want to see you swim. Right?" Ignoring Jake's nonsense, Derrick enlisted support from the others.

The girls nodded. Dustin shouted, "Right!"

"All right. Guess I have to get in sometime."

Jake went to the far end of the pool before shucking his baggy tank top and glasses. The boys hauled themselves up on the side of the pool to watch the demonstration. Darlene held her breath as Jake dove in, releasing it when he surfaced and began to freestyle swim toward them.

"Wow! Look at him go!" Dustin and Derrick cheered. Joanna and Darlene exchanged another glance.

Jake touched the wall, wiped water down his face with one hand, and smiled, blinking in their direction. Darlene suddenly realized that he couldn't see them clearly without his glasses.

"Do the butterfly for us?" Derrick asked.

Nodding, he immediately lunged away again, lifting his body from the water in tremendous forward surges. At the far end he flip-turned and breaststroked back. He was not even breathing hard when he stopped before them to ask, "Satisfied? I don't want to try the backstroke now; might run over somebody."

His four students were properly impressed. "Will we be able to swim like that soon?" Derrick wanted to know.

"Someday you will, if you work at it."

"How much longer will you be, Jonah Kelvin?" came Dora's voice from the sidelines. None of them had noticed when she arrived.

"Not long now." Jake turned in the direction of her voice.

"Did you say we could have some playtime?" Joanna asked pointedly.

"Yup. I figured on throwing you around some." He startled them all by lunging at Derrick, who tried to escape, but was caught by one foot and pulled, very carefully, into the water. Dustin shouted in terror. . .and made certain he was the next victim. He latched onto Jake's neck in an attempt to dunk him, his pale little body glowing against his teacher's brown back, but Jake played and swam as though he carried no burden at all.

Darlene and Joanna watched the boys play, wishing they could join in. The thought of being picked up by Jake sent shivers up Darlene's spine. She shook her head at the idea. *I'm probably too heavy for him to lift.*

When Dustin tired, his mother wrapped him in a towel and allowed him to watch from a lounge chair on the sidelines.

Jake challenged the girls to a splashing contest and kept them at bay until Derrick joined their force. The outnumbered instructor finally sank underwater and emerged at the far end of the pool, shaking his fist defiantly at the giggling girls.

Joanna half-floated in the water, waving her arms dreamily. "Darlene, this swimming lesson idea is a good one after all. I had no idea Jake was such a hunk—" She suddenly gave a little squeal, "Oh! Something grabbed my foot!"

Jake surfaced behind her, water cascading down his face. "School's dismissed, pupils. Head for the dressing rooms."

"Already?" they chorused, gratifying their teacher.

Jake swam to the deep end to retrieve his shirt and glasses from a bench near the women's dressing room door. Darlene and Joanna, wrapped in towels, met him there. His faded red tank top clung to his still-wet body, and water trickled in rivulets down his legs. He wore swim trunks instead of the skimpy exercise suits worn by most of the men in the pool.

He whipped on his glasses as they approached. "I wasn't sure if that was you," he admitted quietly. "See you at church tomorrow. You all did well today."

"Thank you, Josiah Kyle," Darlene smiled, suddenly feeling reckless. She stepped closer to him. "We had fun."

"Did you?" His magnified eyes quizzed her. "I did, too. Good evening, ladies."

To Darlene's confusion, when he stepped past her his cold arm brushed against hers. Water droplets from his arm now sparkled on her arm. She pressed one hand to the place. Had he done that deliberately? If so, it was the first time her amateur flirting had produced any kind of reaction from him.

Joanna examined her face suspiciously. "You sure you're just friends with Jake?" she muttered.

Darlene blinked. "Yes, why?"

Joanna shrugged and headed for the showers. "Well, he did grab my foot instead of yours."

six

Swimming lesson days soon became the highlight of the week for Jake's four students—with the possible exception of Darlene, who counted the days until her next riding lesson. Jake showed unending patience with each of his pupils, bringing them along at a steady pace, careful never to compare them to one another. As the summer progressed into autumn, his increasing workload prevented him from spending as much time at the Althorp home as had been his wont, but the swimming lessons helped keep him in touch. Also, each Sunday he joined the family for their noon meal, his "payment" for the swimming instruction.

He hated to cancel even one swimming lesson, for the calendar told him his time was quickly running out. He was likely to be deployed again over the holiday season, and Darlene would be leaving for Bible college soon after the new year began.

Jake was not a man to hide from his feelings, but some feelings could not be faced lest they become more real. The fact that he was deeply in love with a seventeen-year-old girl was one fact he preferred to ignore and deny—even to himself. Men had lost their military careers over lesser evils.

Occasionally, in weak moments, he allowed himself to dream of her. . .of a long, thick golden braid, sea blue eyes, skin like white silk, a smile like sunshine. He recalled the richness of her voice; even when lifted in anger her voice held a timbre that set it apart, and she seldom lost her temper anymore. Her quick mind, her diligence, her childlike delight in animals, her loving spirit—even her tendency to speak and act without forethought endeared her to him. Her little-girl ways contrasted oddly with her strapping figure, but Jake loved her all the more for them.

Such daydreams were dangerous, however, making it difficult for him to keep his feelings hidden from her, or from anyone else who might be watching him closely. Long hours he spent praying for deliverance from this passion for the daughter of his dear friends, but so far the Lord had not seen fit to alter his feelings—in fact, his love for Darlene only increased over time. Perhaps it was best that they would soon be separated for several months. When Darlene returned from college she would no longer be a minor; this thought relieved some of Jake's burden.

One Sunday in early October, Dora popped a question at him over dessert, "Jeremiah Karl, would it be possible for you to get one day off next week? I have a big favor to ask of you."

"Maybe." He gave her a noncommittal smile. "More information, please."

"Well, I'm sure you've heard us talking about our home-school support group's big field trip to Kentwell Hall, the Tudor mansion where they re-create the past." His nod encouraged her to continue. "Well, one of the group's fathers was planning to go along as a helper, but now he finds he has to work that day, and I was hoping you might be interested in filling in for him. All you'd have to do is videotape the children as they do their activities."

"What about Don?"

Don leaned back in his chair, shaking his head. "Wish I could go, but I've got a conference that week. Can't miss it."

"We thought of you because of your history and teaching background," Darlene told him. "I think this will be a really fun field trip."

"Sounds like it. What day is it?"

"A week from Tuesday, from early morning to late afternoon. We're doing the farmyard day, so we'll be outside most of the time. Pray for good weather," Dora said. "Darlene and I are making costumes, and I'm sure we'll have enough sheets to make one for you, too."

"Sheets? Are we wearing togas?"

"No, but we use old sheets and curtains to make our clothing. It's cheap," Darlene explained. "Let me show you." Rushing from the room, she returned a moment later with some shapeless garments. "These are Derrick's trousers—see the drawstring? And this is his shirt—no buttons, of course. He'll wear this hat," she plopped a floppy brown object on her brother's head. "And we made ponchos out of an old blanket in case it gets cold."

Jake examined the crude garments. "Thought you could sew better than this, Darlene," he teased.

She snatched them away. "Of course I can. These are just for one day, so there isn't much point in putting a lot of work into them. People back then didn't have good-fitting clothing."

"I take it we'll be among the peasant class, not the nobility."

"So you're coming?" Her face lit up.

"If I can get leave."

"Oh, good! Mom, we'd better measure him for size. Are you sure we have enough of the brown stuff for trousers?"

"Let's go find out. Derrick, you're in charge of cleaning up in here today, and Dustin, you will wash."

The boys groaned, but set to work, bickering constantly. Don set the boys straight while the women dragged Jake into the front room where the sewing machine had been set up.

While her mother dug through piles of fabric, Darlene busily set to work measuring Jake's arms. She wrote down the number, then turned to regard him again. "What else do I need to measure, Mom?"

"His chest, waist, inseam and outseam. Oh, and his wrists."

"Lift your arms a few inches, please." Darlene hummed while she wrapped the measuring tape around his chest, but Jake noticed that her long white fingers were shaking. The pink and white flowered turtleneck she wore flattered her figure, and a well-worn pair of blue jeans accentuated her long legs.

"Now your wrist." Their fingers brushed as she worked.

She was all business until the time came to measure his inseam. Flushing, she handed the tape to him, "Um, will you hold this end, please?"

Totally straight-faced, he asked, "Where do you want me to hold it?"

Dora turned to glare at him, though her eyes twinkled. "James Kincaid Edgewood! You know very well what to do. Stop tormenting the child."

Jake obediently held the tape in place, and Darlene measured to just below his knee, then around his calf. "Thank you." He barely heard her little, muffled voice. When she stood up her face was scarlet.

Jake touched her shoulder. "I'm sorry, Darlene. That wasn't kind or polite of me."

She nodded shortly, refusing to meet his eyes. "Mom," she turned away to address Dora. "I just thought of something."

"What's that, dear?"

"Didn't they say no one should wear glasses to Kentwell Hall?"

"Yes, they did, as a matter of fact." Dora grinned roguishly at Jake. "Now would be a good time for you to get contact lenses, Jonadab Kyle."

His brows lifted. "You did it. Kyle is my middle name."

Dora blinked in surprise. "You're kidding! After all these months. . .haven't I called you Kyle before?"

"Not that I've heard. You've still got to guess my first name, though. And, to bring back the former subject, maybe I just will."

He turned back to Darlene, who was staring at him. Meeting those beautiful blue eyes of hers always gave him a jolt, and this time he barely concealed his reaction. "Are you finished?"

"No, I forgot to measure your head for a hat."

He bent over, offering the crown of his head, and Darlene quickly wrapped the tape around it. "You might want it higher than my eyes," he suggested, peeking up at her over the top of his glasses, which she had knocked askew. A lovely aroma of floral soap wafted from her, along with the feminine scent that was purely Darlene's.

She repositioned the tape with shaking hands. Feeling her gentle touch on his hair, he closed his eyes. At last the tape fell away, and she scribbled an unintelligible number on her pad. Jake's eyes popped open, and he pushed his glasses back into place.

"Done," Darlene stated and marched away.

ᴥ

Jake did get the day off, and his costume was completed on time. Early Tuesday morning he arrived at the Althorps' door, ready to be dressed up. Dustin, already costumed in baggy breeches, shirt, and vest, opened the door for him and shouted, "Hey, where're your glasses?"

Jake grinned. "Howdy, urchin. I got contact lenses. Don't yell, you'll wake the neighbors."

Dustin dragged him into the kitchen, where Jake was amused to see two peasant women bustling about, packing lunch into a pillowcase. "Oh, good, you're here," the shorter peasant woman stated. "Dustin, show him where his clothes are and let him get dressed. Oh, and don't forget, we're supposed to speak Tudor English! Jake, do you like hard-boiled eggs?"

"Yea, verily, Mistress Dora." Jake followed a snickering boy from the room.

Jake's woolen breeches fit surprisingly well, but his shirt was tight across the shoulders, making the sleeves too short. He solved that problem by pushing them up to his elbows. Unfortunately, the vest was also too tight, so he loosened the laces until he could breathe. His woolen socks itched, and the open-necked shirt offered little wind protection should the weather turn sour, but he shrugged. "Guess I can rough it for a day."

Dustin and Derrick laughed at the sight of him, happy to see him looking as silly as they did. Darlene pouted to see how poorly his shirt fitted, and tried to pull it together at the neck. Happy to let her pull him about however she wished, he endured this patiently.

In his eyes she looked adorable in her kirtle and vest made from an old blue sheet. Her clothing was too baggy to be flattering, but the color intensified the blue of her eyes, and her white cap framed her sweet face.

"Well, we are certainly a sight to behold," Dora commented when they all stood in the entryway, ready to leave. "I look round as a tub of butter in this rig, and you look like a scarecrow, Jedediah Kyle." She shook her head. "I thought you measured his arms, Darlene. Why are his sleeves so short?"

Darlene could only shrug, embarrassed to admit that she had hardly been able to read her own writing.

"Well, it will give us ladies a thrill to see that manly chest of yours all day." Dora winked at Jake. "Maybe that was Darlene's whole idea."

"Mother!"

Kentwell Hall turned out to be everything the Althorps might have wished for and more. The schoolchildren, ranging in age from seven up to Darlene's seventeen, were divided into groups that moved between locations to work at household tasks, laundry, chopping vegetables for pottage, painting with homemade paints, and woodworking, which included chopping firewood for the bakery ovens. Jake divided his time evenly between the stations, careful not to let his partiality for Darlene show.

After a lunch of vegetable pottage, fresh rolls, and whatever supplemental foods the families had brought along, there was time for games, archery lessons, and exploration. Dustin and Derrick shot several bulls-eyes apiece and looked for a new activity, but Darlene's arrows kept dropping limply to the ground instead of heading for the target. She wanted to give up and follow her brothers to the pigsty, but Jake took over her instruction, insisting that she try until at least one arrow hit the target. He positioned her fingers on the bow and arrow, reaching around her to aim. His matter-of-fact manner irked her, but it also helped her concentrate on the task at hand. At last, she sent a creditable missile into the bale of hay, barely touching the outer ring of the target. The watching mothers clapped, and Darlene felt a glow of accomplishment.

"You did it," Jake praised her, and for a moment Darlene thought she saw a gleam of pride in his eyes. He felt proud of her? It was a new thought which hardly had time to formulate before he was bending over another archery student, positioning the boy's fingers just as he had positioned Darlene's. No, she was silly to think he felt anything special for her. She was just another student to this natural-born teacher.

"Darlene, come here," Joanna called and beckoned from across the field. Darlene obeyed, following her friend to the smithy. "You have got to see the blacksmith! He is a total hunk," Joanna gushed, unmindful of her wholly un-Tudor speech. They stepped into the brick and clay building, where a good-looking young man pounded an enormous horseshoe at an anvil. The girls struck up a conversation with the bearded blond smith, discovering that his name was Clem, that his family had been smiths for several generations, and that he had no use for the king's latest wife, Anne of Cleves.

Joanna, frustrated that he would not be moved from his Tudor role, finally flounced away in defeat. Derrick entered the smithy and stood beside Darlene. "Dar, they've got Suffolk Punch horses here. I'll show you. Come on." Neither of them noticed when Jake slipped in behind them with video camera rolling.

"We've fine cart horses indeed, mistress. The lad speaks truth. Have ye work for Clem this day—a horse to shoe?" the brawny smith inquired, stroking his golden beard.

"No. . .nay, I have none. I admire your workmanship," she chose her words carefully.

"Admire to thy heart's pleasing, mistress. Mine eyes are also well-pleased." Clem lifted one significant brow, perusing her figure slowly as she walked out of the shop. "Thy sister she is?" he inquired of Derrick.

"Uh-huh. . .I mean, yea, uh, verily," Derrick stammered.

"A stout and comely wench indeed," Clem commented behind one hand. "Be she betrothed?"

Derrick looked blank. "You mean, does anyone want to marry her? No way! She's only seventeen."

Clem's eyes boggled. "Not yet betrothed? What ails the eyes of the men in thy village?" He gave Jake a mocking look, then turned his attention to his work.

Outside, Derrick pointed in the general direction of the pastures. "That's where the horses are. I want to go back and watch them feed the pigs. Oh, say, that reminds me. Wait till you hear what that guy in the smithy said about you!"

Darlene tried to look unconcerned when Derrick related the blacksmith's comments, but a hot flush colored her cheeks at the words "stout and comely wench."

"What a thing to say! He's got nerve!"

Derrick snickered at her reaction, and Jake smiled.

"What are you smirking about, Josiah Edgewood?"

"Naught ails my eyes, mistress," he drawled. "Yon smith's remarks will make our videotape most entertaining."

"Oh, no! You didn't!" Darlene flew at him, gripping the front of his vest, knocking him back a step.

Careful to keep the camera out of harm's way, he shrugged. "How was I to know he'd say a thing like that? The tape rolls, and whatever happens is what I record."

"Oh, Jake, please edit out that part! Don't let anyone else see it!"

"Don't you like being a 'stout and comely wench'?"

She pounded one fist against his chest. "Stop it! I'm not fat! . . .am I?"

He couldn't resist those pleading eyes. "I'm sure he didn't mean you were fat. Stout means 'strong and healthy' in the old language. And comely means 'lovely.' "

She took a deep, shaky breath and loosened her hold on his vest. "It does?" Warmth radiated from his sturdy body. His deep brown eyes surely must see into her heart and know all about her silly infatuation—yet he still looked calmly at her, holding his camera under one arm. Either he was blind when it came to girls, or else he didn't want to encourage her.

"Hey, you guys! It's time for group pictures in front of the great hall!" Dustin bellowed across the barnyard through cupped hands. "Where's Derrick?"

Darlene spun to yell a reply, "At the pigsty." She beckoned to Jake. "Come on. We don't want to miss the pictures."

Jake followed at a more sedate pace, cradling the video camera. He stopped once to take and exhale a deep breath.

seven

"What are you writing, Darlene?"

Darlene slammed her journal shut and stared up at Jake with dilated eyes. "N-nothing. I—I didn't hear you coming." It was an accusation.

He joined her on the gnarled tree roots. "I didn't sneak. You were miles away. Where's Dustin?"

"Up a tree somewhere, and François is undoubtedly down a hole somewhere."

"Your mom told me you three were out on the common, so I tracked you down." His dark eyes flickered over her, then away. He picked a stalk of grass and used it to whistle through his thumbs. Recent rains had brought a touch of green back to the common. Today, at least, the tree trunks and roots were dry enough to sit upon.

"I thought you had to work today." Plucking a blade of her own, Darlene tried to make a whistle, but hers wouldn't work.

"I did, but we finished early. I hate working Saturdays. We had a late flight yesterday and no time to debrief afterward because of meetings and such, so we had to go in today." He whistled again, and François came bounding through the tall grass, curious about the strange noise. Whining, the dog thrust his wet nose between Jake's wrists while he blew.

Darlene rolled the dog over and scratched his belly to distract him. Jake blew one short blast on his grass whistle, then dropped his hands. François leaped up, ears alert, to stare suspiciously at the man.

Jake chuckled and ruffled the dog's ears. "Dirty trick, eh?"

"How soon are you leaving for Turkey, Jake?" Darlene couldn't look at him while she asked.

"Tuesday. You know, this might be my last deployment to Inçirlik. It looks like the other squadron will be taking over our mission in Turkey before long, and we'll take their place at Aviano."

Darlene looked blank. "Aviano?"

"Aviano Air Base, Italy. Operation Deny Flight. Patrolling Bosnia." Jake tossed the grass at the dog, stretched out jean-clad legs, laced his fingers behind his head, and leaned back against Darlene's tree, a venerable oak called the "Ship Tree" by the boys. "That should ease our deployment schedule a bit."

"Unless we get involved in the war in Bosnia," Darlene observed.

"There is always that possibility." Jake closed his eyes.

Studying him, Darlene wondered how she could ever have overlooked his overt masculinity. A woolen pullover emphasized the breadth of his chest. She had once thought his face plain, but now she recognized the character traced in its strong lines and admired the smooth golden tone of his bronzed skin. He hadn't shaved that morning; those black whiskers would undoubtedly feel like sandpaper. He hadn't put in his contact lenses either, but she rather liked those black-framed glasses now.

Jake felt her eyes upon his face and suddenly felt scruffy and unappealing. Opening his eyes, he scratched his cheek with a sound like sandpaper and wondered why Darlene's eyes danced with laughter.

François resumed his rabbit hunt. A gust of wind sent crumpled leaves spinning overhead and made Darlene shiver in spite of her coat. The whining roar of jet engines disturbed the peace as a huge C-5 cargo jet lifted off from the RAF Mildenhall runway, raised its landing gear, and receded into the blue distance. Darlene ignored it; living in Holywell Row, she was accustomed to hearing and seeing jets at all hours; but Jake's eyes followed the jet until it disappeared. A deep sigh expanded his chest.

Darlene had a sudden notion that she would fit perfectly right there, snuggled up against his side with his arm wrapped around her shoulders. She could imagine the texture of his brown sweater, the throbbing beat of his heart, the hard muscles beneath his warm skin. . .

Embarrassed by her thoughts, she concentrated on producing a sound from her grass whistle. After several futile attempts, she threw down her grass in disgust. "Are you eager to go to Turkey?"

Jake leaned forward to pick a wide blade of grass, smoothing it between his fingers. "No. Why? You eager to be rid of me?"

"Don't be silly. You're like part of the family. We'll miss you terribly."

"Come here. I'll show you how to make a whistle." He held up the thick blade. "See? Stretch it tightly between the knuckles and the bases of your thumbs, then blow." He demonstrated a low, buzzing whistle, then held his hands up to her face. "Try it."

She placed her lips against his thumbs and produced a creditable whistle. Eyes alight, she turned to him. "I did it!"

He let out a short laugh. "Now make your own." He placed the blade between her thumbs and arranged it for her. His fingers were warm, just as she had imagined. A whiff of shampoo tickled her nose as he leaned closer; he smelled clean and masculine. "Pull it tight. Now blow."

Her sour whistle brought François bounding back, glaring at her in disgust. Flushed with triumph and a touch of some unnamed emotion, she beamed happily at the dog. "I did it, Beau-Beau!"

Jake chuckled. "He noticed."

Darlene practiced while the poodle whimpered and licked at her hands, begging her to cease and desist. Jake finally took pity on him and removed the grass from Darlene's hands.

"What are you doing?"

"Ending the music lesson. I've created a monster." He gave her hand a little squeeze, then leaned back against the tree. With an indescribable feeling of euphoria, Darlene leaned back beside him. The wind whipped roses into her cheeks and nose, but warmth flooded her heart.

"When are you leaving for college?"

"In January, if all goes as planned. I've finished all but two classes now, so there shouldn't be a problem." She couldn't keep the note of pride from her voice. After all, she had worked hard to graduate early. Why shouldn't she be pleased with herself?

"When do you do all this schoolwork?"

"While you're doing air force work, of course. I don't sit around and watch soap operas, you know. I'm presently completing a research paper on sea battles of the War of 1812."

"I'd like to read it when you finish."

"All right."

He drew up one knee and rested an elbow on it. "I'll be deployed until after Christmas. They try to let the married guys be with their families for the holidays."

Darlene didn't know what to say.

"Doesn't look like I'll be back before you leave. You'll keep practicing your swimming, won't you? Looks like there won't be anymore lessons. I think all of you could join the base swim team at anytime. You're ready."

Darlene nodded. "What about a lesson today?"

"I've made other plans for this afternoon." He grinned, but Darlene was too disappointed to suspect anything.

"Oh. Well, maybe I'll take Dustin and go swimming without you."

"No, you won't. You're coming with me. I've signed the two of us up for one last riding lesson—with your folks' approval, of course."

Darlene dropped her journal and nearly hugged him. "Oh,

Jake!" She could only wave her hands around in excitement. "When do we go? Is it time?"

Jake remained seated against the tree, staring up into its branches. "It's so peaceful here; I hate to leave. Maybe we'll forget about riding. You could drop grapes into my mouth and fan me."

"Fan you? Aren't you just about frozen?" Hopping up, Darlene tossed an acorn at him, hitting him squarely in the stomach. "You're nuts! Come on, lazybones."

That got his attention. He sat up, brandishing the acorn. "Nuts, indeed! You realize, of course, this means war!"

"You've watched too many Looney Tunes!" Darlene ducked, but not soon enough to avoid a direct hit. She ran for cover. Placing her notebook on a stump, she began to collect ammunition from the ground while hiding behind the "Cradle Tree."

A fusillade of acorns rained upon her from behind. "Stop it! I'm not ready yet!" she protested, firing back with a will.

"You seem ready to me!" He caught her "bullets" as quickly as she fired them, making her stamp her foot in frustration.

"I can't throw as hard as you can. It's not fair!"

He grinned. "You started this."

She charged, pelting him with acorns as fast as she could throw them. Most of them went wide, but a few bounced off his sweater before he could catch and return them. He held his ground, watching her come. The girl was the picture of health, flushed with excitement, eyes aflame. One of his shots zapped her on the side of the head, and she doubled over, clutching the spot. She was now only ten feet from his position, and that hit must have stung.

"Are you all right?" Remorse tinged his voice. "Sorry I threw so hard." He approached her to offer comfort. She waited until she could see the whites of his eyes, then let loose with a handful of acorns, snickering at the success of her ploy.

"You rascal!" He laughed, grabbing her wrists to prevent

further assault. "Drop them, now!"

"Surrender?" she asked, wrinkling her nose.

"It appears that I have the upper hand, woman." He lifted her wrists, both gripped easily in one hand, and shook them to demonstrate. "I call the terms."

Breathlessly she waited, fascinated by the situation. The wind lifted the dark hair over his brow; his glasses slid down his nose. "You are hurt; there's a red spot on your temple." His free hand lifted to caress the bump.

Darlene's eyes closed as his fingers lightly brushed strands of hair from her cheek. She unconsciously turned her face toward his touch.

His grasp on her wrists suddenly relaxed, allowing her to pull free. He pushed his glasses into place and stepped back, combing through his short hair with his fingers. He looked disturbed. "Truce."

Dustin raced toward them across the grassy field, tripped over François and fell headlong, then hopped up to run again. "Is the war over?" he mourned, panting. "Why didn't you tell me you were gonna fight?"

Jake's frown relaxed. "Not a war—just an indecisive skirmish."

Darlene brushed loose hair from her face again, feeling for the little lump he had found. "Indecisive, my foot! You were outmaneuvered." She fell into step at Jake's side. "We're going to have a riding lesson today—our last one before Jake leaves for Turkey."

Dustin began to complain about being deserted, but the other two tuned him out, absorbed in private thoughts.

❧

Always before Darlene had taken group lessons, which were less expensive. It felt odd to be one of only two students, the other student being Jake, of course. Libby was their instructor.

Jake was assigned to ride League, one of the more advanced mounts. Darlene headed for Willa's stall, but Libby stopped her. "The boss wants you to try a new horse today, Darlene. Pickett is in the last stall in the back stable. He's already saddled and bridled for you."

Darlene felt her heart pound with a mixture of excitement and trepidation. She had once seen Pickett shy severely and dump his rider. Would she be able to control him? The gray gelding was usually well behaved, but he was unpredictable.

She patted Willa's Roman nose as she passed the mare's stall. "Sorry, girl. I've got to ride Pickett today."

Pickett waited for her, his head thrust over the half-door, his short ears pricked toward the riding arena. He was patient while she fiddled with the various straps on his bridle and tightened his girth, but he nearly ran over her on the way out of the stall. Darlene gained new appreciation for Willa's good manners.

Jake was already warming up League out in the arena when Darlene climbed upon Pickett's back. He felt strangely thin to her, being a much lighter horse than massive Willa. He also stepped out much more briskly when she cued him to walk, nearly running over Libby. "Darlene, you must direct him more carefully than that. Don't allow him to be rude."

After twenty minutes of walking, sitting trot, rising trot, and reining Pickett through patterns, Darlene began to feel more at ease. She was not happy with the way Libby blamed Pickett's faults on his rider, but she did realize that she was supposed to be controlling him, not the other way around. The wind had risen during the past hour, roaring through the huge chestnut and eucalyptus trees surrounding the arena and making it difficult for Darlene to hear Libby's commands. Libby didn't seem to understand this problem, and berated Darlene for not paying attention.

Once Pickett shied at a blowing leaf, but Darlene controlled him efficiently, making him continue to trot in a wide circle. He was a wily creature, well accustomed to taking advantage of novice riders. He rolled his eyes, flicked his ears, and snorted testily, but this time, at least, he didn't get away with his foolishness.

"Good work, Darlene," Libby admitted. "For a moment there I was certain you would take a fall."

Darlene glowed with self-satisfaction. She patted Pickett's furry neck when Libby went to instruct Jake for a few minutes, leaving her to practice alone. "You may be ornery, but you're kind of fun to ride."

Jake was cantering his mount on both leads, and Darlene couldn't help being jealous when she saw him take League over a few small jumps. It would be years before she reached that level at the rate she was learning.

At last, Libby told them both to cool their mounts. One of the exercise girls came out of the office, signaling and calling that Libby was wanted on the telephone. "You two keep cooling your horses. Make another two rounds of the field at a slow walk. Margie will help you untack if I don't return in time."

Jake headed League across the field toward Pickett so they could walk the laps together. Darlene smiled at him, but couldn't take her attention from Pickett for long. The gelding was itching to cause trouble now that Libby had gone. "I wish she hadn't left us alone," Darlene admitted when Jake was within earshot. "I don't trust this creature for a minute."

The words were barely out of her mouth when disaster struck. Weakened by recent drenching rains and high winds, a large branch broke from one of the trees surrounding the field and landed upon the arena's perimeter fence with a tremendous crash. The horses nearly jumped out of their skins with fright. League threw up his head and shimmied sideways, whinnying with fear, but Pickett leaped right out from under Darlene and tore across the field toward the gate, bucking and twisting. She barely stayed with him, clinging desperately to the side of the saddle, until he reached the gate and flew over it. Darlene landed on the near side of the gate, flat on her back; Pickett landed on the far side of the gate, still running.

League stopped near Darlene, sliding on his hocks in a shower of mud like a well-trained cow pony. Jake leaped from the saddle and squashed through the ankle-deep mud to Darlene's side. League trotted a short distance away, then turned to watch the humans, his eyes wide, nostrils flaring.

"Darlene! Darlene, are you all right?"

She lay completely still on her back in the mud, her long braid dangling into a puddle. Her eyes were open, wide and shocked. "I. . .I think so."

He began to feel her arms and legs for fractures. "Can you move your legs?"

She bent her knees slightly. "Yes. I think I just got the breath knocked out of me. Where's Pickett?"

Jake muttered something unintelligible.

Libby came running, ducking beneath the gate rails. "What happened? Where is Pickett? Don't move her; she may have internal injuries!"

"I haven't moved her. Your horse headed for his stable when that branch broke loose." He pointed at the offending limb. "I don't think she's broken anything. You go collect League; I'll take care of Darlene."

Libby obeyed his authoritative voice. Poor, bewildered League was only too happy to be caught and cared for.

"Can you sit up, sweetheart? I'll help you."

Darlene enjoyed the vast difference between the way he spoke to her and the way he had spoken to Libby. "I think so. Oh, Jake, I'm a mess! Look at this mud!"

The entire back side of her helmet, jacket, and jodhpurs was plastered in thick, ice-cold, aromatic sludge, but Jake took no notice. He wrapped an arm around her shoulders as she sat up, and helped her to her feet. She clung weakly to him. "I feel weak and shaky, like my legs will give way," she said, her voice tremulous.

He held her tightly, his cheek pressed to hers, his glasses

knocked cockeyed. Their safety helmets conked together when he tried to draw her closer. "You scared the daylights out of me, sweetheart. I thought I'd killed you!"

She pulled slightly away. "You? It wasn't your fault; it was that silly Pickett. I knew he was looking for trouble, but I think he got more than he bargained for." She gave a short chuckle. Jake's frightened voice had given her courage.

"So much for my special treat for you," he grumbled.

Darlene patted his back with a filthy hand. "It was a special treat. Thank you. I learned a lot today. Don't blame yourself for my spill; it could have happened anytime."

"Guess we'd better get out of this mud, eh?" Jake looked down at their boots, submerged to above their ankles. "Good thing you bought yourself some real riding boots; your hiking boots would have been ruined by this."

Darlene tried to move, but her legs were too weak to pull her feet out of the sucking mud. "I think I'm sinking. This must be quicksand."

With one fluid motion, Jake lifted her into his arms and marched out of the riding arena, stepping carefully over the gate rails Libby had left down when she led League away. Darlene was too surprised to speak, but she quickly wrapped her arms around his neck to help him balance. He carried her all the way back to the office before setting her carefully down.

"Better?" he asked, only slightly breathless.

"How did you do that?" she sputtered. "I can't weigh much less than you do!"

"You've lost weight recently, or I probably couldn't have done it," he admitted. "You're pretty slim these days, kid."

Libby quickly came to help them scrape off and clean up enough to drive home. She was humbly apologetic. "The boss will kill me when she hears I left you alone on Pickett," she groaned. "Please come back and try riding him again. I swear I'll do a better job teaching you next time!"

Darlene smiled kindly, though her teeth chattered. "Don't worry, Libby, I'll be back. I've got to show Pickett that he can't treat me that way and get away with it! A little mud never hurt anyone, after all. At least I had a soft landing pad." She patted her soggy backside.

Dora was horrified when Jake and Darlene appeared on the doorstep like a pair of shivering, bedraggled mudhens. "I'll go straight home and shower, Dora," Jake told her. "Don't worry about me. You take care of this muddy urchin. She got badly shaken up today, I'm afraid."

"You're welcome to use our shower, Jake," Dora protested. "The boys will be crushed if you don't stay for dinner. We have so little time left to spend with you before you deploy."

Weakening, Jake glanced down at himself. "Guess I'm not too filthy to wait in the kitchen while Darlene cleans up."

"Of course not. I'll get some of Don's clothes for you. They'll be big, but not that bad."

Showered and fresh, Darlene sat in her room and listened to the water run while Jake showered. There was something intimate about having him take a shower in her home, in spite of the fact that her entire family was present to chaperone them. She flopped back on her bed and petted François absently.

"He carried me, Beau. I never thought he'd be able to lift me, but he did." She smiled dreamily. "He said I'm slim. Slim! Me!" The smile widened as she stretched lazily.

Dressed in baggy sweats, Jake laughed, joked, and teased the boys as usual that evening at the supper table. If he looked at Darlene with unusual tenderness, only Dora noticed. After dinner the family played several rounds of trivia games, which usually ended as battles between Don and Jake. Tonight was no exception, and the others took sides. Derrick and Darlene backed Jake; Dora and Dustin backed Don. Don declared himself the winner when Jake had to ask Darlene the name of the author of Little Women.

Jake conceded defeat. "I've never read that book, and I've never seen any of the movies," he confessed as they put the game back in its box.

"Louisa May Alcott is one of my favorite authors! How could you, with all your education, not know her name? We have the movie with Katherine Hepburn as Jo," Darlene informed him. "Do you want to watch it?"

"Tonight? No," he shook his head. "I. . .uh, I need to talk with your dad." He turned to Don. "If you have time, sir."

Don's curiosity was aroused. "Of course. Right now?"

Jake nodded, glancing around at their intent audience. "In private."

Don waved his hands. "Out! Everybody out! Avast ye, me hearties! Off with you! This is man talk."

The children obediently scattered, though evidently prickling with curiosity. Dora followed, ordering them to shower and to bed, though she longed to be in on the closet conference.

When the voices faded upstairs and thumps could be heard overhead, Don smiled at Jake. "This is as private as it gets around here."

One side of Jake's wide mouth twitched. "I didn't intend to be so mysterious."

Don waited.

Dropping his head forward, Jake ran all ten fingers through his hair, destroying its smoothly combed wave. "I need to tell you that. . .that things have changed. I mean, I've changed."

Still Don waited.

"I don't know how to say this, Don. I know it's crazy; she's too young for me, and we're going to be parted for months while she's at college, but I. . .I want to marry Darlene."

Don laced his big fingers together. "Dora has suspected as much for some time, Jake."

Under his kindly gaze, Jake felt blood rising to his face. "I don't know how she knew, but. . ." he shook his head. "Can't fool that woman."

"You want to talk about it?" Don asked.

"I don't know what to do. She plans to complete a college degree! That will mean years apart, years of waiting." Misery tinged his voice. "I can't ask her to give up college. A brain like hers would be a terrible thing to waste."

"Why couldn't she attend college after you're married? There are extension courses available on this base, and you might be stationed near a good college on your next assignment. If she wants a degree badly enough, you could work it out."

Jake's mournful expression lightened slightly. "You think so?" Then it fell again. "But it's far too late to change plans for this school year. She'll be leaving for college in a few weeks and I won't even be here to tell her good-bye."

"Does she know how you feel about her?"

"I haven't told her, but she must suspect."

Don restrained a smile. "A while back she told Dora that she could not imagine you ever falling in love. I believe they were discussing your girlfriend at the time."

Jake winced. "Yeah, then there's Teri."

"Where does that lady fit into the picture?"

"Teri is my adopted sister's best friend. She kind of took me under her wing when I first joined the Edgewood family, and I guess she still considers me her chick. She's like that, sort of maternal and managing—in a nice way. I love her; she's a jewel, really."

"Well, I can't tell you how to choose a wife, and I can't guarantee my daughter's reaction to the idea of marrying you. She's very young and has big plans for the future."

Slumping back in his chair, Jake nodded. "I think she likes me, maybe she even loves me in a way, but I'm not sure she'd go for the idea of marriage. She doesn't really understand the concept of love yet."

"You're undoubtedly right. I wish I could be more encouraging. I'm sure she cares for you, as we all do, but I believe you would be wise to give her time to mature. Perhaps next summer. . ."

Jake took a deep breath, but said nothing, so Don continued. "Let her experience some of the ups and downs of life. If she meets and marries another man, it means God has other plans for you both. But if she comes through college heart-whole and fancy-free, she just may see her old friend Jake in a new light."

Staring intently at the tabletop, Jake nodded. It was the wisest plan, but he didn't like it. Not one bit.

eight

Jake dropped by Monday night to wish the Althorps an early "Merry Christmas" and to tell Darlene good-bye. He put on a cheerful face, but Dora saw through his mask in a heartbeat. She gave him a motherly hug before Darlene came downstairs. "Don told me all about it, you sweet boy, and we're with you all the way."

Blushing, Jake returned her hug fiercely. "Thanks, Dora. You're a keeper."

"I hope you'll be calling me 'Mom' someday," she murmured.

Poor Jake only blushed harder. "She doesn't know, does she?" he asked hopelessly.

"We've never said a word! How could you think so? I've kept your secret all these months; why would I spoil it now?" She pulled his head down and kissed his cheek. "Merry Christmas, Jeffrey Kyle." Releasing him, she asked hopefully, "Is that right?"

He shook his head. "Nope. Keep trying. You'll get it eventually."

"Can you stay for a while?" Entering the room, Don shook Jake's hand heartily. "You could challenge me to another trivia game."

"Not tonight. I still have to fold laundry and pack." Jake looked sorely tempted.

"Derrick is out tonight, but Dustin and Darlene are home. I think they're reading." Don stepped to the base of the stairs and called his children. "Jake's here to say good-bye."

Dora squeezed his hand, feeling the tension he was trying to hide. "Just be yourself, dear," she advised. "The months

75

will pass, and you can always write letters and call her."

He nodded, looking sheepish.

Dustin pounded downstairs first, followed by François, then Darlene. "Aren't you staying for a while?" she asked, looking upset.

"Can't. I've got to pack. I spent most of the weekend here, and now I'm paying for my procrastination." While talking to Darlene, he held off Dustin's attempt to tackle him. "Just came to collect some good-bye hugs and wish you God's best at college."

Darlene's eyes filled with tears. "It doesn't seem possible that I won't see you for months and months. You'll write to me, won't you?"

"Sure I. . ." he stopped to clear his throat. "Sure I will. You'll answer, won't you?" One hand on top of Dustin's blond head, he fought to stave off the boy's attack.

"Yes." A tear spilled over. This was not the romantic send-off she would have liked to give him.

Jake finally grabbed Dustin in a bear hug, wrestled him to the floor, and blew a raspberry on his cheek. Writhing frantically, Dustin screamed and hollered in disgust, then dissolved into laughter. "Serves you right, you knucklehead," Jake told him fondly. "Won't give a guy a moment's peace! I'll see you next year, so beware!" he shouted after the boy's retreating form, chuckling softly. "What a goofball."

He glanced up at Don and Dora and rose to his feet. "You'll tell Derrick good-bye for me?"

"Of course, dear, but with less violence than your good-bye to Dustin!" Dora gave him one last hug. "Call us on Christmas Day, all right? We'll want to hear from you."

Don shook his hand, then gave him a quick hug. "Take care, son. See you in a few weeks. Darlene, why don't you walk Jake to his car?"

It was an innocent question. Darlene didn't see the color flood back into Jake's brown cheeks; she was busy putting on her shoes and coat.

She linked her arm in his as they descended the steps. It was another windy night; scattered clouds wisped quickly across the starry sky. Jake wondered how much he should say and silently prayed for wisdom.

"I wish you could be here for Christmas," Darlene sighed. "We've never had a Christmas together. It's hard to believe we've only known you for ten months; you're like family. How much longer will you be stationed in England?"

"Another year. Single guys only get two-year assignments; married guys get three-year tours. I could extend for a year if I wanted to, though."

"I hope you do. We would miss you terribly."

They had reached his car, but Jake made no move to unlock it. He stared at the ground. "Are you still feeling stiff from your fall?"

"A little. I really wasn't hurt much; the mud made for a soft landing. I need to go riding again, but it won't be the same without you there."

She felt him take a deep breath. "No, it won't be the same for me without you either."

"Is something wrong, Jake? I get this feeling you're trying to work up nerve to give me bad news or something."

"No, you already know the bad news. I'm just being a coward about saying good-bye. I'll miss you, Darlene. You don't know how much."

Touched, she gave him a hug, and was surprised when he hugged her back tightly. All she could feel was the pressure of their two coats, but his breath was warm on her cheek.

"May I kiss you good-bye?"

She was surprised, but delighted that he asked. "Of course you may, Jake." She kissed his cheek, feeling the day's growth of beard with her lips. Warmth filled her heart; her knees felt weak. She waited with closed eyes for the long-anticipated touch of his lips upon her cheek. He need never know that his kiss meant far more to her than a simple farewell gesture.

To her utter surprise, his return kiss landed on her lips, or nearly. He missed on the first try. Her mouth dropped open just in time for him to find it with his; the unexpected passion of his embrace shocked and thrilled her.

"Jake?" she breathed when he released her.

He caressed her cheek with a trembling hand. "I shouldn't have done that, but. . .you're so sweet! Can you forgive me?"

Still stunned, she could only nod.

"Good-bye, Darlene." He unlocked his car, climbed in, started the engine, and drove away while she stood gaping after him, waving dazedly.

nine

Darlene knocked on the bathroom door. . .again. "Brittany, if I don't get into the shower soon, I'll be late! Please hurry! Rick is picking me up in forty minutes."

The door opened, and the other girl emerged, sour of expression. "I'm hurrying! Don't be so bossy; the shower belongs to me as much as it does to you."

It hadn't taken three days in the college dorm for Darlene to decide that making four women share one shower stall and toilet was a ridiculous idea. She liked her roommate and suite mates, but the girls fought over that shower on an almost daily basis. Being the youngest and most easily pushed around of the four, Darlene nearly always got the short end of the stick. It annoyed her, but she had no idea what to do about it.

Dorm life was her least favorite part of college. Many of the other girls came from less conservative homes and enjoyed music, literature, and conversation that had appalled Darlene at first. She had expected better at a Bible college. On the other hand, her classes were stimulating and challenging, chapel services were inspiring, and her male classmates interesting. After her first few weeks of deathly homesickness, she had recovered to the extent of seldom thinking of home and family at all. Studies, her job at the local YMCA, and outings in the company of friends occupied her mind, leaving little time for letter writing.

Spring had arrived in this little North Carolina town, bringing thoughts of romance, and at present, romance had taken the form of a junior named Rick McGann. Blond and dashing, Rick had pursued Darlene since the first time he sat beside her

in psychology class. Lately they had paired up on group outings, and their names were being linked in people's minds.
Tonight, for her eighteenth birthday, Rick planned to take her
to a Shakespearean play in the nearest city, then dinner. Her
first real date!

Darlene thought about Rick as she showered. He was out-
going and charming, tall and thin with puppy-dog brown
eyes. He was absolutely nothing like Jake, and in some ways
this annoyed her. He had no interest in sports. Darlene made
herself swim laps at the campus pool each afternoon, but Rick
would never join her. She admitted to herself that no stunning
muscles could possibly hide beneath Rick's baggy shirts. He
never exerted himself to develop any. Still, he was attractive.

Darlene paused to consider her thoughts. *I sound like I'm
trying to defend him,* she realized. *But against what?* Evading
her own question, she finished dressing, blew her hair dry,
and French-braided it. Lately she had begun wearing makeup,
at Brittany's urging, and she liked the way the color brought
out her eyes and lips. Her silky dress clung in all the right
places, and the neckline showed a tantalizing quantity of soft
skin.

Would Jake want to kiss her again if he could see her now?
One finger lightly touched her lower lip, then she jerked it
down. Frustrated, she wondered, not for the first time, if she
were really in love with Rick at all.

"Oh, Darlene," Brittany cooed. "You look fabulous! Rick
will be drooling all over his bib tonight, I predict. You'll have
to tie his hands down. That dress is you, honey, let me tell ya!"

The Shakespeare comedy was delightful, dinner splendid
and delicious, and the company superb that evening. Rick had
obviously spent top dollar to impress her. Darlene was
touched. . .and amazed that he would go to so much trouble.
While he talked, her eyes traveled over his handsome face,
crisply waving hair, and graceful hands. Was this gorgeous
man really her date?

In the midst of her stare, Rick's eyes locked with hers, and she saw his face redden and his hands tremble. She immediately returned her attention to her meal, her lips curved in a smug little smile.

"Happy?" Rick asked as he helped her into his compact car that night.

"Of course—and very full!" she chuckled. "Thank you for a wonderful birthday, Rick. I can't remember the last time I had so much fun!"

He flashed her a boyish smile. "The evening isn't over yet! We've got a drive ahead of us."

They discussed school events, stories from their childhoods, and music during the drive home. Then Rick parked in a dark area of her dorm parking lot. She could barely see his face, but she could hear and feel him breathing. She picked up her purse and reached for the door handle.

"Wait. I'll walk you to the door in a few minutes. I was hoping. . .well, I've wanted to ask, may I kiss you, Darlene?"

He sounded nervous. After that wonderful evening, how could she say no? One kiss couldn't hurt anything. "Yes."

She felt his hands grasp her shoulders, then one slid up to hold her chin. His lips touched hers lightly, then with increasing confidence. Darlene expected to feel the way she had felt when Jake kissed her, but instead she only noticed that Rick's breath smelled of Italian dressing and his lips felt wet.

Breathing faster, Rick pulled her close and kissed her again. Feeling rather left out of the experience, Darlene kissed him back and found that her minimal response fired his passion. With a little moan he began to kiss her cheeks, her neck, her collarbones, "Darlene, you're so beautiful!"

"Rick," she said seriously. "I need to go inside now. It's nearly curfew."

He dragged himself away, trying to see her eyes. "You can't go in yet; we just got here, and I've planned this evening for weeks. Just a little longer. . ."

She felt his fingers stroke her throat, then wander toward her dress's low V neck. Grabbing the door handle, she abruptly opened her door and climbed out, leaving her date floundering over her empty seat. "I want to go in, Rick. I said you could kiss me, not. . .not touch me like that."

His face looked pale in the car's interior light. He said nothing, but climbed out to escort her. At the dorm entrance, he grabbed her elbow. "I'm sorry, Darlene. Guess I presumed too much. I thought you wanted it as much as I did."

He looked so mournful that she relented slightly. "I forgive you. But I don't think we ought to go out together alone for a while. Maybe just with groups again."

She watched him walk away like a puppy with its tail between its legs and felt a little bit sorry for him.

Back in her dorm room, she thought over that short adventure in his car while washing her face. It was good to wash away his moist kisses, scrubbing until her face and neck felt clean again. *I didn't feel this way when Jake kissed me. Is there something wrong with me, or is Rick simply the wrong man?*

"Have fun?" Brittany sat up in bed, looking groggy.

"Yes, it was a wonderful play, and we ate in this fabulous restaurant, all candlelight and soft music."

"Rick really pulled out all the stops, I guess. How come you're in so early? I didn't expect you for hours yet." Brittany squinted at her clock radio.

"It's after eleven, Brit."

"You won't see me coming in from a hot date before curfew, I can tell you that much! Rick dated Tamara Quinn last year, and she never came in before the wee hours. You're such a baby, Darly."

"Am I?" Darlene stared at her reflection critically. Rick had dated Tamara? That was news to her.

"Oh, by the way, you got a phone call earlier. It was a man, but I didn't catch his name. Said he'd call back tomorrow."

Darlene turned to stare wonderingly at her roommate. "A

man? Sure it wasn't my dad again?" Her parents had given her a birthday call that morning.

"I'm sure. He said his name, but I don't remember."

"You could have written it down." Darlene turned back to the mirror.

"I would have, but he said he'd call back. G'night." Brittany rolled over.

Was it Jake? Squeezing her eyes shut, Darlene fervently hoped so.

❧

Darlene had to work the next day. Rick also worked at the YMCA day care, but their paths seldom crossed, for they worked with children of different ages. During lunch break, while Darlene's small charges napped, Rick managed to slip away for a quick visit, catching her alone in the break room with her mouth full of sandwich.

"Darlene, I need to talk with you. . .about last night. I want to tell you how sorry I am for the way I acted. . .there's no excuse for it, but I. . .it won't happen again. I—I care too much about you to let it happen again."

Darlene finally swallowed and was able to contribute to the conversation. "I forgive you, Rick. I couldn't sleep for a long time last night, and I spent the time studying Bible passages about relationships and about how we're to behave toward one another. I need to apologize to you, too. I didn't exactly intend to lead you on, but I think I did anyway, which was thoughtless and selfish of me."

He sat beside her on the bench, one hand propped on a bony knee. "What do you mean?"

"I've been looking for romance instead of friendship, when friendship is what I really need. We don't know one another very well yet, Rick."

Rick struggled to follow her reasoning. "We've been seeing each other for two months now."

"Yes, but only on outings. How can a real friendship develop when the only time we're together is on dates or in class? It's so artificial."

"Well, what do you want me to do?" Taking her free hand, he gently rubbed the back of it with his thumb. He looked determined to accomplish the task, whatever it might be.

"Some members of my debate class discussed courtship as opposed to dating a few months ago. I thought it was interesting at the time, but didn't think it could apply to me. Now I'm beginning to think it might not be a bad idea."

Rick shook his head. "What do you mean? Isn't dating the same as courtship?"

Darlene found his touch distracting, bringing back memories from the night before. A little shudder ran up her spine, and she sat straighter. "Not the way they described it. The idea was for men and women to form friendships within the safety of a group, kind of like we did. Then, if a real attraction began to form, the man would approach the woman's father for permission to court her. He would get to know her family, spending time with her in the home environment, and take her to meet his family as well."

Rick lifted one eyebrow. "Don't you think that would be difficult, under the circumstances?"

"Yes, but not impossible. You could talk to my father on the telephone. Anyway, after a period of courtship, the couple would plan marriage, or else decide not to marry, in which case, since there had been no physical involvement prior to a commitment, it shouldn't be a painful breakup."

Now both blond eyebrows raised in disbelief. "You're kidding me, aren't you?"

"No, I'm not. I don't see any point in romance unless there is real intent for the future—marriage, I mean. A man who is seriously interested in a woman would be willing to make an effort to approach her parents, I'm sure."

"You're sure. That's just swell. Look, Darlene, I'm only twenty-one years old, and I have another year and a half of college ahead, then graduate school. You're, what, just eighteen? Marriage is a long way down the road—it has to be! I don't mean to be flippant, but get real! Grow up! This is the nineties, not the nineteenth century! There are other kind of relationships, you know. We can just be. . ." He shrugged in frustration, "romantic friends, I guess you'd call it."

Darlene's voice trembled, but she barreled ahead. "But what goal would you have for our relationship?"

"Goal? Why does there have to be a goal? Can't we just enjoy life while we're living it?" He gripped her shoulders and gave her a gentle shake, then tried to pull her close. Unheeded, her lunch bag fell to the floor. "Look, I think you're gorgeous, Dar; I'm crazy about you. I think about you all the time, so much that I can hardly study! But, honey—"

Darlene pushed at his arms and shook her head to cut him off. "No, there's no future for us, Rick. Face it! Apparently what you want from me is a good time, including unlimited kisses and hugs in a dark car, with no strings attached. That's not what love and romance are about. Not for me."

He released her and stood up, his passion turning to anger. "Okay, so we've figured out what I want from you, have we? Now how about we work on figuring out what you want from me?" Rick's voice rose. "It's clear to me now, babe. You're one of those uptight chicks who comes on strong with the sexy looks and unspoken promises, then gives a guy the iceberg treatment and the 'but I never meant to lead you on' once you've got him on your string and he tries to collect. I didn't figure you for that kind of woman, Darlene."

Darlene gasped in fury. "How dare you? Why, I never. . ." Sudden recognition of the truth in his accusation cut off her protest. "You know what I said last night about us not dating for a while? Make that permanent." Rising, she rushed back to the activity room, leaving the stunned and angry young man behind. Rick kicked her abandoned lunch bag across the room, then dropped upon the bench with his head in his hands.

ද

Darlene had no chance for a good cry until after work. Swarms of children at the Y, crowds of strangers on the bus, chattering girls in the dorm hallways—no privacy at all. Thankfully, when she reached her dorm room Brittany was out. Dropping her purse on her desk, she flopped across her bed and let herself relax.

The tears refused to come. After a minute she sat up, flipping her frazzled braid over her shoulder, and began to weigh Rick's shortcomings on a mental scale. She shrugged. He was no great loss.

Whenever Rick talked with her, his eyes would frequently drop to scan her body and legs, or lift to caress her hair. At first she had found this habit annoying and rude, but before long she had become accustomed to it, even flattered by it. Handsome though he was, she did not yearn for his touch, and it gave her a feeling of power to know that he desired her while she was immune to him. Fresh anger at his shocking accusation swept over her, and this time she refused to see his point of view. "The creep," she muttered, shuddering anew at the memory of his fervid caresses. *Dad would have been proud of the way I ran from temptation last night,* she told herself, ignoring the truth of the matter.

A wave of homesickness swamped her. How she longed for a good talk with her mother! Often in the evenings when she needed a good talk, she would ask her mother to brush her hair, and Dora always knew what that meant. They had shared some wonderful times, revealing inner longings and fears—though at the moment Darlene couldn't recall even one of those longings and fears. None of them compared to the trials of the present day. What would Mom and Dad think of Rick? As a prospective son-in-law he would have been found sadly wanting. His commitment to the Lord was superficial at best, making little impact on his behavior and goals.

Of course, my own relationship with God isn't the closest. She sighed. Last night while studying her Bible, she had confessed her selfishness and sinful desires concerning Rick, but today she felt as remote from the Lord as ever. *It's as though I have the walk and the talk down pat, but the spirit and fire are missing.*

She heard the pay telephone in the hallway ring twice before someone answered it, then a knock at her door. "Telephone, Darlene. Are you in there?"

"Yes! I'm coming." Darlene flew to the phone, her heart in her throat. "Hello?"

"Darlene? This is Jake."

He sounded so close, yet there was a slight delay between their voices. "Jake, oh, it's good to hear your voice!" Her own voice nearly squeaked. She closed her eyes to savor the ecstasy of the moment.

Kathy, who had answered the phone, imitated Darlene's squeak to her roommate, and giggles filled the hallway before their bedroom door closed.

"I tried calling last night, but you were out. Just wanted to wish you a happy birthday. Eighteen, right?"

"Yes! Finally." Now her voice was trembly.

"Getting old, huh? I've still got a big lead on you."

"You're twenty-seven now, aren't you?"

"Yup. Don't remind me."

"Silly. That's not old. How have you been? Are you in England or in Turkey?"

"England. We won't be deploying to Turkey anymore. The whole squadron is home right now for the first time since the end of the Gulf War. We had a party to celebrate the occasion. It won't last long though. Things are heating up in other places. You know what I mean."

"Oh, Jake, I don't want you to go there! It's too dangerous! That F-16 pilot got shot down, and I—"

"Better not talk about it, sweetie. How's school going?"

Deflated, she stammered, "Um—uh, fine. I'm doing fine. Did Mom tell you I'm competing for an academic scholarship that would pay next year's tuition?" She winced. What a brag-gart!

"She did, and I'm sure you'll get it. I'm proud of you. Are things going better in your debate class?"

"Yes, a little better. I'll never be a good debater, but I'm learning."

He chuckled. "I've always found you to be a gifted debater. Short on logic, perhaps, but always willing to debate an issue."

She bridled, but grinned. His teasing brought her back to earth, and she could speak normally again. "All right, knock it off! That's what I meant when I said I'm learning. It's not always easy to find a basis for my opinions, but I've got plenty of 'em."

"I won't argue with you there."

"Smart alec." Then, "How are the Shackletons doing? I heard about the excitement when their baby was born."

"Yeah, that was an adventure. They're doing fine. The little guy is growing fast. You know they'll be leaving for good this fall."

"I was afraid of that. At least I'll see them this summer. Where are they going?"

"To Seymour Johnson Air Force Base, not far from where you are. Shack will be an instructor at the RTU. It isn't a great move for his career, but it will be good for his family life—no more deployments."

"He almost missed their baby's birth, didn't he? I hear you nearly got to be midwife," Darlene teased.

"Well, it wasn't quite that bad. I called Polly to tell her that Peter was stuck up in Scotland and had to take a train home, and she told me she was in labor. All I did was pick her up and take her to the hospital. Shack made it home in plenty of time; the baby wasn't born till the next day."

"Mom told me she has baby-sat the little guy a few times. I can hardly wait to see him. Where are you right now? At home?"

"Yeah, why?"

"I just wondered. I've never seen your home."

"Not much to see, only a small two-room flat."

"In town?"

"No, on a farm. It used to be hired-hand quarters. Very spartan."

"Do you have your own furniture?"

"A few things. Most of it came with the flat. Looks like something from the seventies—you know, olive-green fixtures, orange shag carpet, gold curtains. I put in a shower right after I moved in. All it had was a bathtub."

Darlene made a face. "You poor thing! No wonder you're always at our house."

"Yeah, this place doesn't feel much like home. But then, your folks' place isn't the same without you there."

"Will you be eating with them tonight?"

"No, not till tomorrow. They went somewhere today, on a tour or something."

"I guess it's past dinnertime there, isn't it?"

"Yup. Already ate my TV dinner."

His soft voice brought memories flooding back, and suddenly Darlene longed to be with him, to hold him close. She could have clung to him forever.

"Jake, I miss you." Jake always had an open ear, and he knew the Lord so well. He might be able to tell her what was missing in her relationship with God—but how could she explain her lack, her loneliness over the telephone?

"I miss you, too, sweetheart." His voice sounded as husky as hers. "It's been a long winter, and spring is dragging. I'm glad you're working hard at college and having some fun times too."

There was a question in his voice; she was sure of it. Was he wondering about her date last night? "I went to a Shakespearean play last night—*All's Well That Ends Well*. It was great."

"Sounds good."

"I went with a guy named Rick. We went out to dinner at an Italian restaurant afterward."

"Yeah? Don't have many of those around here."

There was jealousy in his voice! All at once she wanted to clear away his doubts. "It was a nice dinner, and I enjoyed the play, but I'm not going to date Rick anymore."

"Any particular reason?" He sounded guarded.

"He wants romance, but he doesn't want any real commitment, and I don't see the point to that kind of relationship. It may be popular in the nineties, but I prefer old-fashioned ways. Jake, would you take a girl out, spend lots of money to entertain her, then expect her to let you kiss and hug her all you wanted with no strings attached?"

Silence for a moment. "No, I wouldn't."

She felt vindicated, and jabbered on, "I didn't think so. I didn't know he had that in mind until last night. He's a cute guy with lots of personality, but I didn't want him kissing me all over. It made me very uncomfortable."

Silence again.

"Jake? I've made you uncomfortable, haven't I? I'm so sorry! I've got to learn to keep my big mouth shut! I just needed to talk about it to someone, and then you called. . ." She felt guilty, though she wasn't sure why. A sob caught in her throat.

"Darlene, don't cry. I'm. . .I'm. . .well, I don't know what I feel. I wish I was there, but maybe it's a good thing I'm not. I might punch a fresh kid's lights out and get myself in trouble."

"Would you do that? I always wanted a big brother to beat up bullies for me." That ought to get a rise out of him if he had any romantic interest.

"Yeah, well. . ."

His noncommittal drawl disappointed her. She blurted, "Don't worry. I'll keep out of trouble the rest of this year. I've already decided not to date anymore; I'm planning to concentrate on schoolwork and build friendships with the girls in my dorm."

"Sounds ambitious and wise. I'll be praying for you, Darlene. This is a difficult time for you, a time of deciding what you want in your future, or more importantly, what the Lord wants for your future."

"Yes, I do want to please Him. I wish I. . .Jake, would you talk with me about God when I get home this summer? I feel like I need to talk and share some things with someone, but there is no one here. . .like you. I can't explain what I mean over the telephone though. Would you?"

"I'm honored that you would ask me." His voice sounded unusually deep.

"There's no one like you, Jake." Darlene put her heart into her voice, wishing to communicate how much she appreciated his friendship.

Once again he was puzzlingly silent. Then, "You're. . .very special to me, too, Darlene."

"Well, I must be running up an outrageous phone bill for you."

"It's worth every pence."

"You will be there when I get home this summer, won't you? I'll be back in mid-June."

"I can't make any promises. I should be here for at least part of your summer vacation."

"Oh!" She sounded desolate. "You'll make time for us, won't you?"

"Darlene, you know I will." He sounded almost impatient.

"Isn't your sister coming to visit you soon?"

"Yes, in August."

"With Teri. Mom told me about that."

"Yes, with Teri, and with Leigh's husband, Reg."

"Bet you can hardly wait." Now she sounded jealous.

"I'm sure I'll be happy to see them all. But Dar, Teri. . .is just a good friend."

"Does she know that?"

"I wrote to her recently and explained my feelings. I thought at one time that I might marry her someday, but I never will. It's never been. . .serious between us. I mean. . .it just isn't."

"You're not like Rick, you mean, expecting kisses and hugs from your dates."

"I guess that's what I mean. I am human, Darlene. Don't make me a paragon of virtue. You, of all people, should know better."

He must be thinking of that good-bye kiss. Darlene grinned wickedly but kept her voice serious. "It's just hard to imagine you. . .well, you know. You're so good, and so self-controlled—most of the time."

"I think this conversation has gone far enough. You be good, you hear me?"

"Yes, big brother, I hear you, and I'll be a good girl. Thank you so much for calling me! This is a great birthday present."

"Good. See you in a few months."

"All right. Good-bye, Josiah Kyle."

"Good-bye, Darlene Joy."

Click.

He was gone. For those few minutes he had seemed so near—and he was so very dear! Dreamily she hung up the phone and wandered back to her room. Oh, Jake! No thought more coherent than that one crossed her mind all day, but one thing she knew: That telephone call had been a turning point in her life.

ten

Jake dropped back on the bed, hands clasped behind his head, and looked longingly at the telephone, hoping it might ring. The Althorps had his phone number here at the Italian hotel, but Darlene never called him. Jake rubbed his aching forehead, wishing he could relax. Even in his dreams he could see the switches and television screens of his jet's rear cockpit, and he frequently woke himself up making imaginary radio calls aloud. Since NATO had finally decided to begin bombing key Serbian positions in Bosnia, the deployed Strike Eagle aircrews had enjoyed little rest. There had been no time for sight-seeing in Vienna or anywhere else.

He and Peter Shackleton had originally been scheduled to return to Lakenheath three weeks earlier, but war had changed their plans. An experienced pilot like Shackleton could not be spared, and Jake had found, to his surprise, that he was one of the most experienced Wizzos in the 494th Fighter Squadron. A recent influx of new blood—young officers—had lowered the squadron's experience level dramatically.

One week to go, he reminded himself, wondering what Darlene might be doing at the moment. She had been back in England for a month. Jake longed to telephone the Althorps, but it was getting late, and he feared making a pest of himself. He had spoken with Darlene several times recently, but none of their conversations had been satisfying.

Reaching out one hand, he groped on his bedside table until his fingers grasped a worn letter, dated many weeks earlier. He scratched his nose, feeling for glasses that were not there, and began reading it again, frowning slightly.

Dear Jehoiada Kyle,

*I hope your deployment is going well. I can't help
worrying, but I know you won't take unnecessary
risks. . .will you? We're all doing well here, finishing
the school year and preparing for summer. The boys
can hardly wait for the squadron tour you've
promised as a field trip for our home-school group.
It will be one of the highlights of their year, I assure
you.*

Jake smiled. Dora was making sure he didn't forget his
promise. She needn't have worried.

*Darlene has plane tickets for June sixteenth. Her
last few letters have sounded homesick. Has she
written to you lately? She asks about you in every
letter and telephone call. Don says I'm not to med-
dle, but I want to tell you that she is no longer interested in that Rick fellow from her psychology class.
She seems to have lots of male friends, which
pleases me, indicating as it does that she has
matured emotionally.*

*Guess what—Darlene won the Henderson
Scholarship, a complete academic scholarship
which will pay for her entire next school year! Don
and I are so proud—*

Jake crumpled the letter with a wistful sigh. Happy for
Darlene and proud of her though he was, deep inside he had
hoped she would not receive that scholarship. This made certain that she would be away for another school year, a full year
this time. He began to figure on a mental calendar. It was now
late July. He would arrive home next weekend, have five days
more or less free, then his family would arrive for a visit. If
Darlene returned to college in late August as planned, he

would end up with barely three weeks to court her. . .it was contemptible to begrudge time with his sister, brother-in-law, and Teri—but grudging was exactly how he felt. He was disgusted by his selfish feelings, yet he could not deny them.

Teri. How could such a nice person be such a headache? He dug in the drawer for another letter and unfolded it, hoping it would read differently this time. He skipped over much of the letter, but one section deepened his frown.

> *After I complete my degree and you finish your military duty, I don't think we'll have any trouble finding openings in a foreign mission field. The difficulty will be in determining which field God has prepared for us! I get so excited when I think about our future, serving the Lord together wherever He calls us!*
>
> *Dearest Jake, I can't imagine a future without you. My heart yearns toward the day we will be together always. I'm counting the days until my plane takes off, until I see your face again.*

Jake winced. Obviously she had not understood the meaning of his last letter. He had tried to be kind and tactful, but all that sugar coating must have obscured his message: We are only friends. And in a few short days she would arrive in England, evidently expecting a romantic idyll.

"Too bad I won't still be deployed," he muttered, wishing for the coward's way out.

There was a knock at his door. "Jake? You in there?"

"Yeah." Jake opened his door to Craig Medwin, one of the newest Wizzos on this deployment. "What's up, Winner?"

"Have you eaten? Some of us are going out for pasta."

A moment's consideration, and Jake answered, "Be right there."

Peter Shackleton, Medwin, and a pilot, Todd Swansea,

waited in the lobby. Together the men walked down the street to find an open restaurant.

Conversation around the table lagged at first. The two pilots quietly discussed their latest flights without mentioning potentially dangerous details. The other two men studied their menus. Homesickness ate at the married men and Jake, while Medwin, who was a bachelor, was simply fatigued and bored. He had hoped to paint the town red during this deployment but found that war cramped his style.

After the waiter served their meals, Peter and Jake bowed their heads in silent thanks. Swansea ignored them, but Craig Medwin suddenly observed, "You're not like most religious guys I know."

One of Jake's black brows lifted. "What do you mean?" He broke open a roll and reached for the butter.

"I don't know. Like, you make me feel uncomfortable sometimes, but it's not like you think you're, like, better than me. Maybe what I mean is, like, I feel uncomfortable with you because you really are good, and you seem to enjoy being good, and I can't relate to that. Does that make any sense?"

Swansea nearly choked on his fettucini. "None at all."

After sifting through the "likes," Jake did understand. He glanced at Peter, who nodded encouragement. "I don't enjoy being good for the sake of knowing I'm good, Win. I enjoy being good because I know it pleases God, and more than anything in this world I want to please Him."

"Why?" Medwin was curious. "So you can go to heaven?"

"Because I love Him. I wouldn't want to go to heaven if I didn't love God, because heaven is where He is. What most people can't or won't believe is that living for God is far more fulfilling than living for pleasure. He takes care of all my needs, so I don't have to worry or fret about anything. I'm free to enjoy life. People who seek pleasure find it always just out of their reach, while people who seek God find that He fills their every need."

Swansea concentrated on his food. Medwin looked incredulous. "That's nice, I guess, if it works for you."

This time Peter spoke up. "It can work for anyone. God's promises aren't for a few select people. Anyone can know Him the way Jake and I do."

"Yeah, but it isn't that simple. God makes a lot of demands, and He doesn't always keep His promises." Bitterness laced Swansea's voice, surprising his companions.

Medwin's eyes moved from face to face. "What kind of demands? Give up all the fun in life? Join a monastery?"

"You aren't required to make any changes in yourself first. Lots of people think God wants us all to become monks before He'll accept us, but it's not that way. He'll take you just the way you are; He loves you just the way you are. Getting rid of sins is His job, not ours," Peter explained. "We're only required to confess our sinfulness and give Him the chance to do His work. He'll never force anyone to submit to His will; we have complete freedom of choice. Of course, a true believer shows a difference in his life. Once you're God's, you want to please Him with the way you live, and He gives you the power to do it."

"What God offers is an exchange: your old life for His gift of new, eternal life in Christ Jesus," Jake added, feeling thankful for Peter's presence. "Why cling to something we can't keep—life here on earth—and reject His offer of eternal life? Can anything be more important than the opportunity to know the God Who created the universe? Think about it!"

"Too cosmic for me," Medwin shook his head, still looking puzzled. "And too complicated."

Swansea regarded Peter and Jake with hostility. "Maybe we'd rather keep a sure thing than gamble on a pipe dream," he snorted. "Knock off the religious talk, would you? I'm losing my appetite."

Medwin shrugged good-naturedly. "What with Jake and Shack being role models for the rest of us, this whole squadron will be psalm singers before we get back to the 'Heath."

"Say, wouldn't that be something?" Jake grinned.

With a disgusted but friendly epithet, Medwin changed the subject.

Jake's smile faded as he recalled his own words. "More than anything in this world I want to please Him." *Is that true?* "He takes care of my needs, so I don't have to worry or fret. . ." *Ouch! What exactly have I been doing? Yup, worrying and fretting, big time.*

He stared blankly at his pasta. *How can I expect God to work through a hypocrite like me? No wonder Win is confused and Todd is antagonized.*

Peter stopped by Jake's room that night, obviously wanting to talk. He flopped back in a chair with a casual air. "So, what did you think of our talk at dinner?"

Jake sniffed in wry amusement, feeling awkward. "Kind of bombed, didn't it?"

Peter shrugged. "Maybe. Maybe not. It's hard to tell what God might use. At least we tried to answer Win's questions."

Their conversation soon turned to easier subjects. "Yeah, I gotta call Polly and let her know when I'll be home, now that we finally have a moving date set. She's been quietly panicking, thinking she would have to arrange our move back to the States all by herself."

"I'm afraid to set my heart on any date; the powers that be have a history of changing their minds."

"I'm trusting that this one will hold true. I've got to get back to out-process. No one in the squadron seems to want to accept the fact that I'm leaving for good. I've also got to get home to see my son before he grows up without me."

After Peter had returned to his own room to telephone his wife, Jake pulled out his neglected Bible and dropped to his knees beside the bed.

"Lord, I haven't been trusting You. I've been stumbling along on my own, trying to make my will into Your will. I haven't been fair to Teri or to Darlene—neither of them have any idea what I've been planning and dreaming about, and it's time I let them know where I stand without worrying about my pride. Keeping one girl on a string until I have the other one secured is a low trick, but I've done it. Please forgive me; teach me to trust in You, to deny myself, and follow Your leading instead of my wayward thoughts."

eleven

Darlene's bubbles had all popped, but the bathwater was still warm around her ears as she lay flat in the water with her legs folded on top. Running her fingers through her hair, she swished it around in the water, feeling like a mermaid. It was so good to take a bath or shower whenever she pleased without a lineup of girls pounding on the bathroom door. She didn't care that the tub was too small; privacy was golden.

Washed, rinsed, and wrapped in a towel, she smoothed perfumed lotion over her entire body and dressed with care. Blow-drying gave her hair volume, and hot rollers added billowing curls that cascaded over her shoulders. Today she went overboard on the cosmetics, hoping to create a sensation.

"Won't he be surprised?" she asked her reflection. This was the day she had been anticipating for weeks. . .no, months. Jake's plane was due to arrive at the RAF Mildenhall air terminal in a matter of minutes. Soon he would call, and the whole family would go to meet him. A genuine war veteran! Watching BBC coverage of the NATO air strikes had terrified her, but now that her hero was returning she was thrilled that he had taken part in the strikes.

Crazy plans surged through her head. She envisioned running up to Jake, throwing her arms around his neck, and planting a kiss on his mouth. A fascinating thought, but unrealistic in the extreme. Perhaps he would stare admiringly at her, then pass her by, searching vainly for the old, gawky Darlene. Surely his eyes would spark with interest when he saw her fabulous new outfit. All of her daydreams involved an awestricken, bowled-over Josiah K. Edgewood.

Slipping into her bedroom, she spent a few more minutes

primping, hair spraying, and admiring her full-length reflection. Running her palms down over her hips, she practiced the "sultry siren stare." Not bad! Amazing what makeup, a new hairstyle, flattering clothes, and a touch of self-confidence could do for a woman.

Her family's reaction let some of the wind out of her sails. "You're not going to wear that, are you?" Dora asked bluntly as they all gathered in the entryway.

"What's wrong with it?" Darlene had been surprised by the frequent disagreements she'd been having with her mother. It was disappointing to find that her parents and brothers were unimpressed by her newfound maturity, style, and poise.

"You look like a magazine cover," Derrick stated, looking her over. He had shot up several inches during the winter, and she now looked directly into his disdainful blue eyes.

"Thank you." She softened visibly.

"I meant one of those raunchy hot-rod magazines. You look all paint and varnish. One good rain and you'll melt all over the ground. Ooh! I'm me-elting!"

Darlene bridled, ready to lash back, but Don intervened. "That's more than enough, children." He looked at Darlene. "Are you certain you don't want to change?"

"Dad, not you too!" Darlene rolled her eyes in despair. "What's wrong with what I'm wearing? I chose this outfit carefully."

"With what intent?" Dora spoke through tight lips.

"Did you dress like that at school?" Derrick inquired, honestly curious. "I thought this was a Bible college where they taught—"

"Of course I didn't dress like this for school! It would have been entirely inappropriate. What kind of an idiot do you think I am?"

"A very young one," Don sighed, but she did not hear.

"Brittany, my roommate, helped me pick this outfit out, and I love it! I saved for months to afford it, and I'm going to wear it."

Darlene smoothed her pink leather skirt over her hips and zipped the matching jacket up a few inches. Countless hours of swimming had given her a trim figure, and she intended to capitalize on it. She was not used to wearing tight clothing, but she considered discomfort a reasonable price to pay for looking like a model. Her pink pumps added inches to her height, but they were part of the outfit, and she couldn't bear to give them up.

Don and Dora exchanged pained glances, but dropped the subject. Darlene was old enough to select her own clothing.

"Let's not keep him waiting." Don opened the front door for his family. "He said Pete Shackleton and two other men came with him from Aviano on a KC-10 tanker."

Darlene tried to maintain a cool reserve during the short drive to the air terminal, but she kept relapsing into arguments with her brothers. They were so immature! Dustin insisted that Jake would want to see the new baby rats as soon as they returned home. Derrick wanted to ask about the air strikes. Darlene's plans for Jake's time were too private to share, but she was not averse to ridiculing her brothers' ideas.

She spotted Jake waiting in front of the terminal as they drove up, along with Shackleton and two other men. Arms folded across his chest, Jake stood squarely, expectant eyes on their van. He wore a burgundy polo shirt and snug jeans that emphasized his square shoulders and lean legs. Darlene's heart began to thump with nervous excitement.

Just ahead of the van, Polly Shackleton stopped her car, threw open the door, and leaped into her husband's open arms. Darlene noted that Polly wore yellow leggings and matching tunic sweater, and her hair was simply braided down her back. She looked sweet and beautiful, as always. Peter had eyes for no one else, and would hardly release his wife long enough to load his bags into their car. Darlene saw him bend over the car seat in the back to greet his tiny son.

A knot rose in Darlene's throat. The purity of their love contrasted sharply with the cheapness of her intentions toward Jake. What had she been thinking? Suddenly Darlene did not want to get out of the van. She huddled in her seat, hoping no one would notice her.

Don hopped out to assist Jake with his luggage.

"Doesn't Jake look nice?" Dora asked innocently over the back of her seat. "I wonder what they're discussing out there. Looks like we're giving a ride to that other young man."

Don opened the back of the van to load bags and leaned in to say, "We're giving a ride to Craig Medwin. He lives in West Row. Darlene, scoot over to the middle to make room. Dustin, I've got to put this bag on the seat beside you."

Jake pulled open the van's side door. "Sit with me back here, Jake!" Dustin begged.

Jake climbed into the backseat. "Hi, Darlene! Welcome home. I'll let Winner sit up there with you so he can climb out easily."

"Hello, Jake," she replied stiffly. "Welcome home to you too." Not a word about her new look. No reaction at all. She might as well have worn grubby jeans and a T-shirt, for all he noticed! Relieved, she relaxed slightly. Maybe her outfit wasn't so shocking after all.

A slight, dark-haired man slid the side door shut, then sat beside her. She looked up in time to catch his dropped jaw and stunned gray eyes. "Hel-lo!" he spoke at last, putting a wealth of meaning into the word. "And you are?"

She allowed a ghostly smile. "I'm Darlene Althorp."

"Jake never told me about you. I'm Craig Medwin, known as 'Winner,' and the pleasure is all mine!"

She did not dispute that claim. The van seemed dreadfully crowded. Medwin's shoulder pressed against hers.

Jake leaned forward. "Win, meet Dustin and Derrick, Darlene's brothers. That's Dora Althorp up front, and you met Don. They are Darlene's parents." He put a slight emphasis on the word.

"Pleased to meet you, Craig," Dora smiled over her shoulder. "Are you a Wizzo like Jake?"

"Yes, ma'am." Shifting his weight, Medwin casually draped one arm across the back of Darlene's seat. She could almost feel his eyes scanning her legs. She tugged at her skirt in a vain attempt to make it longer.

"Jake, Reba had nine babies a few days ago. Wanna see 'em when we get home?" Dustin offered eagerly.

"Sure." He answered without really hearing the question. His eyes were on Darlene and Medwin. "How's swimming going?"

"Okay. Our team got third place in the last meet, and Derrick won the fifty-meter breaststroke! I got second in the fifty backstroke."

Jake was properly impressed, proud of his students. Derrick joined the conversation, asking dozens of questions. Jake promised to tell his war stories later that day when everyone could listen. For the present, he turned the subject to the squadron tour he had promised the home-school support group. "Most of the squadron is deployed right now, but I should still be able to give you a decent tour." The boys' eyes glowed with anticipation.

Under cover of their noisy chatter, Medwin leaned closer. "I'd like to see you again sometime, Darlene. May I have your phone number?" She felt his breath down her neck and recoiled into Derrick, who shoved back, not appreciating her problem. Medwin brightened, thinking she had moved closer to him intentionally.

Suddenly, Medwin's eyes widened and lowered to stare at his right arm. A hand reaching around the side of his seat held it in a viselike grip. He cranked his neck around to see Jake's face. . .abruptly removed his other arm from the back of the seat, and subsided into his seat corner, silent for the duration of the drive except when he provided sketchy directions to Don.

Darlene breathed a relieved sigh when they let him off at his house. He politely thanked her parents for the lift, but did not even glance her way. She wondered why he had suddenly lost interest in her, but was too preoccupied to give it much thought. Would Jake sit beside her now? What would he say?

After helping carry Medwin's bags, Jake did change seats, taking his first good look at Darlene as he climbed into the van. He paused, startled. Her eyes, their color and size emphasized by heavy mascara and eye shadow, focused upon his just long enough to read his shock and dismay before lowering to her clenched hands.

Jake had intended to give her a welcoming hug, but the phrase "too hot to handle" flashed through his mind as he settled beside her. Buttery leather against his bare arm, heady perfume from her billowing cloud of golden curls, carefully lacquered pink nails, none of these seemed familiar. What had happened to his Darlene?

Even as he carried on a conversation with Derrick and Dustin, he sneaked glances at her, and pain stabbed at his heart, akin to jealousy. Could this be the same girl who had balked at "making a spectacle of herself" by wearing a racing swimsuit at a public pool?

A trembling gasp escaped her parted lips. Curious, Jake looked closer. Long, blackened lashes fluttered, and a tear left a gray trail as it trickled down her cheek and dropped to her leather lapel. The curve of her cheek and her pouting lips, though they were rouged and lipsticked into vivid hues, were still soft and childish. Jake recalled her uncertain voice and her evident discomfort with Medwin's flirting, and a smile twitched his lips. Whatever had prompted Darlene to turn herself into an oversized Barbie doll, his heart told him she regretted that choice now.

While Dustin and Derrick discussed the finer points of their last swim meet, Jake reached out to gently wipe another tear from Darlene's cheek. Startled, she jerked away, squeezing her eyes tightly shut.

Just then the van pulled into the driveway.

"Bail out!" Don gave his usual order, this time with astonishing success—Darlene unbuckled her seatbelt and lunged for the side door, pushing past Jake's legs.

"What in the world. . . ?" Dora exclaimed, turning in time to see Darlene half-fall out of the van and run up the walkway. One spike heel stuck in a crack between bricks. Leaving the shoe behind, she hip-hopped to the door, dug in her handbag for the key, threw open the front door, and staggered upstairs.

Once in her room, she closed the door, kicked off her remaining pump and fired it at the trash can, whipped off her jacket and skirt, and flung herself across the bed, weeping violently. François, who had sneaked in at her heels, jumped up beside her, whimpering and licking her bare shoulder with a comforting pink tongue. Without pause, in her grief she wrapped one arm around the little dog and hugged him to her, soaking his topknot with her tears.

Outside, the three adults exchanged baffled glances. "Now what was that all about?" Don wondered, giving Jake an odd look.

Dustin hopped down, scooped up the discarded pink pump, and dangled it from one finger. With a wicked grin, he offered it to Jake. "You must find the one maiden with a foot big enough to fit this slipper."

Jake couldn't help but smile, but the look in his eyes nearly broke Dora's soft heart.

twelve

"I don't even know what I did wrong," Jake groaned after dinner that evening. He had divided his attention between the boys all afternoon, fruitlessly keeping an eye and an ear out for Darlene. She had declined to come down for dinner, claiming a headache. The boys were presently watching a videotape in the family room, leaving the adults free to talk.

"It wasn't you, dear," Dora tried to explain. "She's embarrassed, and she's punishing herself, I think. She's been longing to see you, Jake."

Covering a yawn, Jake grumbled, "Whatever. I need to get home and unpack. If she doesn't want to see me, guess I'll head out."

"You'll come for dinner after church tomorrow?"

Pushing back his chair, he moped, "Don't want her to starve to death. Maybe she'll eat if I'm not around." Catching Dora's hurt expression, he amended, "Thanks for the invite, but I don't want to eat you out of house and home. Seems like I'm always sponging off you."

Watching him clear the table and scrape plates into the garbage, she scoffed at that. "Jarvis Kyle, a few meals could never repay all you've added to our family. Your company is payment enough."

"Amen to that," Don agreed.

Jake squeezed Dora's shoulder as he passed her chair, wondering how much longer he would be welcomed into Darlene's family circle. Overtired and depressed, he mournfully imagined Darlene's future husband taking over his place in the family. The interloper would play tennis with Don, build projects with the boys, be teased and mothered by Dora. How

Jake would miss them all! Even Dora's determination to guess his name would be a cherished memory during lonely years to come. And Darlene, his Darlene. . .a black cloud descended over Jake's heart at the thought of all he stood to lose. . .

Don slapped his pockets to find his car keys when Jake indicated that he was ready to go.

"Sure you won't stay for a few games?" Dora followed them to the door. Jake's woebegone look worried her.

Jake turned back. "Not tonight. Dora, you're a treasure. Thanks for everything."

Dora gave him a quick hug. "Wish we could help more, but this is your game."

He gave an inarticulate grunt. "My game, eh? Wish some-one would tell me the rules." It was disconcerting to have people read his feelings so easily.

"Hmm," she lifted one brow, regarding his long face criti-cally. "'Pears to me you already have a rulebook."

After a moment's thought, he gave her a rueful half-smile. "Yeah, guess I'd better spend more time reading it and living it. Tell everyone good night for me."

"I'll tell her."

Minutes later Dora knocked at Darlene's bedroom door. A small thump and scrabbling footsteps told her that François waited on the other side. A long sniff came from the crack beneath the door.

"Darlene? May I come in?"

"Yes." She barely heard the reply.

The door wasn't locked. After a quick glance at the piles of discarded clothing, Dora sat beside the huddled figure on the bed and smoothed the golden curls. "How's your head? Did the aspirin help?"

"Yes, thank you, Mom." A mere whisper.

Dora searched for comforting words. "Jake said to tell you good night. I think he was hurt that you didn't seem happy to see him. He has really missed you." That understatement didn't give away any secrets.

Darlene did not respond.

Dora decided to be straightforward. "Honey, what's wrong? I can't help you if I don't know why you're upset."

The girl began to cry again, her shoulders shaking.

"Darlene, what is it? Please talk to me!"

"Oh, Mama, I don't know. It's just not like I thought it would be!"

Unenlightened, Dora asked, "What isn't like you thought it would be?"

"I wanted to show all of you how much I've grown up, but you all still treat me like a child!" Her voice trailed off into another wail.

"Oh." Dora blinked. "But, Darlene, you are our child. I do see new maturity in you, and so does your father, but you can't expect us to change our behavior overnight. You'll always be our little girl." She reached out, and after a moment's hesitation, Darlene nestled into her arms.

"I'm so confused and lonely! I don't feel like I belong anywhere. I was homesick when I was at college, and now I don't feel comfortable when I'm here. It's all so. . .so different! I almost wish I'd stayed there and worked at the Y all summer."

Dora smiled. "You expected us to stay the same while you did all the changing?"

"I guess I did." A long pause. "I looked silly in that outfit today, didn't I? Brittany told me I looked gorgeous in it, and I believed her. I've been saving it for a special occasion."

Dora didn't mince words. "You looked like a young woman who wanted to turn masculine heads."

Darlene cringed. "Was it that obvious?"

"Yes, and when you succeeded, you didn't like it much, did you?"

"No," the girl whispered. "I've never felt so humiliated. Oh, why did he have to be there and see me? I'll never live this down!"

"Isn't he the one you wanted to impress?" Dora prompted quietly.

Darlene's face crumpled as she nodded. "Did he say anything? About me, I mean?"

Choosing words carefully, Dora said, "He was hurt that you avoided him. He never mentioned the way you looked. He's your friend, honey, and true friends look at the heart."

Darlene considered this, feeling slightly comforted. "Was he really hurt?"

Dora's brow wrinkled. "Darlene, wouldn't you be hurt if he shunned you after all these months apart? He's the same sensitive, lovable man we've known for more than a year now, made of flesh and blood. Men can get their feelings hurt just like women can."

"I never thought I could hurt Jake. He seems so. . .self-sufficient."

Once again, Dora was amazed by her daughter's lack of perception. She sighed deeply, thinking, *he'd better be patient as well.*

Darlene sat up, brushing tangled hair from her eyes. "Mom, what can I do? To make him notice me, I mean? I've never felt shy around Jake before, but now I don't know what to say to him." She reached up to flatten her hair with both arms. "He's so wise and mature and. . .and a man, and I feel like a little girl playing grown-up. At college I had lots of guys as friends. It was fun, and I liked some of them. . .but none of them were like Jake."

Treading carefully, Dora asked, "What was different?"

Darlene appeared to be lost in thought. "It's hard to say. There's something about Jake that I had forgotten until I saw him today. He's just so. . .so good, so. . .oh, I don't know. I only know that as soon as I laid eyes on him, I realized how silly I'd been to imagine he'd be overwhelmed by a sexy dress. I feel so dumb!"

She gave a little shiver, and her hands crept up to grasp her bare arms. "Oh, it was awful! I thought I'd die when he noticed I was crying, and all I could think of was that I had to get away before I made a total fool of myself." A sudden fear made her grab Dora's arm. "You won't tell him, will you? I'd just die!"

"Of course not!" Dora straightened. "I won't say a word. This is our secret." She studied her daughter with wistful eyes, seeing a blooming woman in place of her baby. "Darlene, I have a suggestion for you, if you really want to develop your relationship with Jake."

Darlene was all ears.

"Attracting a man's attention to your body is no challenge. As you've learned, a sexy dress can accomplish that with just about any man. The challenge is to develop love, the marrying kind of love, which I believe is what you want from Jake."

"What do I do? I don't have the first clue how to make a man love me like that!"

Dora figured Darlene was better off not knowing how deeply in love Jake already was. Attempting to win his love would be good for her. "To receive that kind of love, you must first be prepared to give it. You might try asking him about his job, or about his hobbies. I don't think you actually know much about him, his background and interests. By taking an interest in him as a person, you can distract yourself from thinking of him only as a man."

"But jets are so boring to me, Mom. How can I seem interested when I'm not?"

Dora gave her a disapproving look. "If you're interested in the man, you'd better be interested in his career. You can take an interest in anything if you want to badly enough. You'll have a golden opportunity this next week: Our home-school support group is taking a tour of Jake's squadron Tuesday, and afterwards he will reserve the simulator just for our family."

"I know about it, but I'm not in the group anymore."

"I'm sure we can make an exception. You can help watch over the little ones."

"I'm not cleaning Mrs. Hacker's house this week, so I do have Tuesday free," Darlene mused.

After a moment's silent contemplation, Dora asked, "You saw Polly Shackleton today, I imagine?"

"Yes. When did she get back from the States?"

"I think it was Thursday morning. She looks good, doesn't she? I can hardly wait to see how that baby has grown."

"She looked gorgeous, as always. No one would know she just had a baby a few months back. I took one look at her today and knew I looked like a tramp." Darlene hopped to her feet and changed out of her stretch lace bodysuit into a faded nightshirt. "Is Jake coming for lunch tomorrow?" she asked eagerly, already making plans. "I'll try to make up for today."

"Don't overdo a good thing," her mother warned. "Be subtle, if possible."

"Mom!" Darlene protested, but smiled, acknowledging the merit of her mother's advice. "Guess I did overreact a little today."

To her credit, Dora let that one pass without comment.

Darlene scooped up her pink jacket, grimacing. "I don't think I'll ever wear this again."

"It might be salvageable. You could try wearing it with jeans or a flowery skirt. That skirt, on the other hand, has few redeeming qualities."

As Dora made her way to the door, Darlene asked her one more question, "Mom, is Teri Sutton still coming to visit Jake?"

"Jake's sister, brother-in-law, and Teri arrive Friday morning—Derrick is going along on the drive to Heathrow to keep Jake company. Jake took leave from work for the first week they're here to show them local sights, then they'll go up to Scotland for a week without him. I'm planning to ask them all to Sunday lunch next week. Good night, honeygirl."

"Good night, Mom."

thirteen

In church the next morning, Darlene sat with Joanna and several other old friends. She planned to wave and smile at Jake when he entered the sanctuary, and perhaps entice him to sit with her, like old times. To her dismay, he was closely followed from the adult Sunday school class by a strange young woman and never so much as looked in her direction.

"Who is that woman with Jake?" she lost no time in asking Joanna.

"She's Pam Dietrich. Haven't you met her? She's a pilot of one of the big planes at Mildenhall base," Joanna whispered back.

Darlene tried not to be obvious, but it wasn't easy to keep an eye on Jake without turning her head. He shared a hymnbook with the woman and once bent his head to hear something she said. Otherwise he seemed to concentrate on the service.

Darlene tried to focus on the sermon, but, as usual, her mind wandered. *I'm prettier than she is,* she assured herself, but she remained unconvinced. Pam Dietrich was a cute little thing. The type that appealed to the protective instinct in a man. *Few men would feel protective toward an Amazon like me.*

Darlene had dressed carefully that morning, deciding upon a blazer and skirt set with a dainty rib knit shell beneath. The pale peach and blue plaid set off her fair complexion, and the cut hugged her figure while remaining modest. She had curled her hair, but cut down on the teasing and hair spray. The attention she had received from the college-age boys that morning told her that she looked good, but approval from Jake was required before she could believe it.

After the closing song, Darlene checked on Jake again. He stood in the aisle, talking with Polly Shackleton, who held a bright-eyed bundle of baby boy. Pam Dietrich was nowhere in sight. Darlene brightened.

"Polly," she cried. "Welcome home!" Casting a shy look at Jake, she met his gaze and felt herself blushing. "Good morning, Jake." It came out in a mumble.

Polly wrapped her in a warm hug. "It's so good to have you home, Darlene. You look great!"

"I've been waiting to meet your son, Polly. He's beautiful!" She picked up a dimpled fist and let the baby grasp her watch.

"Thank you. Meet John Andrew Shackleton. He's six months old. We call him Drew."

"He has your big brown eyes, Polly. What a sweetie! May I hold him?"

"Of course. In fact, I need to catch Rita Fraser before she leaves. Would you mind baby-sitting while I talk to her?"

"I would be delighted."

The baby was duly transferred. Seating herself on the end of a pew, Darlene babbled softly at the cooing baby, then looked up at Jake's sober face. "Don't you like babies, Jake?"

"Terrible creatures," he stated softly, reaching out to touch Drew's chubby bare leg. "Of course I like babies. You look comfortable with that one."

He stood so close that his trouser leg brushed her sleeve. The room suddenly seemed overly warm. Darlene couldn't look up again, but the baby made a convenient excuse to keep her eyes lowered. "Jake, I'm sorry about yesterday. Are you coming over for lunch today?"

Her heart sank when he moved away, but he sat sideways in the next pew up and rested his forearm on the back. "Do you want me to come?"

"Yes, very much."

He was silent. Worried, she glanced at his face, her eyes

revealing the truth of her words.

"Then I'll come." His expression softened as she watched. She noticed details of his face: a faded scar on one cheekbone, the gloss of his thick black lashes and brows, the places beneath his lower lip where no whiskers grew, the way his contact lenses shifted when he blinked. His dark-chocolate eyes examined her features with equal interest.

Tired of being ignored, the baby reached up to grab Darlene's nose. Diverted, she giggled, and Jake smiled at the cheerful sound.

"Jake?" Pam Dietrich appeared in the aisle beside them. "Are you coming with us?"

He rose politely. "Not today. Thanks anyway, Pam."

Her face fell. "Oh, well, maybe next week." She totally ignored Darlene.

When she was gone, Darlene breathed easier. "Um, friend of yours?"

"You might say that. She invited me to join the singles group for brunch today. I've gone with them once or twice."

"But you're coming to our house instead?" Darlene peeked at him from beneath her lashes.

"No contest. Here comes Polly; looks like you'll have to surrender that baby."

Derrick and Dustin rode home with Jake while Darlene occupied the middle seat of the family van, staring dreamily through its windows. Her parents were discussing church business, so she tuned them out. Romantic hopes swirled through her mind, mingled with fears and insecurities.

Darlene had prepared a Mexican casserole that morning in hopes that Jake would be coming home from church with them. She tried not to watch him eat, but it was difficult to behave normally while he sat opposite her.

"Great meal, Darlene," he praised, folding his napkin. "As always." His eyes were gentle, admiring.

"She hasn't lost her touch whilst slaving over the books,"

Don admitted. "Someone must have trained her well." He winked at his wife, who had risen to carry over her dishes.

"Since you cooked, I'll clean up the kitchen, Darlene," Dora offered kindly. "Are you taking a walk on the common today?"

Jake waited for Darlene's answer, but Dustin cried, "Yeah! I've got a cool new hideout to show you, Jake." Scooting back their chairs, the boys picked up their plates to carry over.

Dora signaled to Don, but he didn't understand. "Think I'll stay home this time," he faltered, blinking at her. She shook her head vehemently behind Jake's head until Darlene looked up. Then she coughed, patting her chest.

"Why don't you go with the boys this time?" she directed Don. "And let Darlene have some time with Jake. They monopolized him yesterday."

Dustin groaned. "But he wouldn't go with us yesterday either! Why can't Darlene come with us on the walk?"

"I don't mind sharing him," Darlene lied, rising to clear the table. "Just give me time to change clothes."

Dora nearly told her boys to stay home and wash the dishes, then realized she was being obvious and gave up. *Lord, I've got to trust You to work this out!* she admitted, berating herself while rinsing dishes. Don offered to wipe them for her, trying to make amends for misunderstanding her signals.

Hands in the dishwater, she leaned her head against his shoulder. "It wasn't your fault, sweetheart. I'm no expert at this matchmaking business. Things seem to be going well today, but I always want to hurry them along a bit."

"Do you think she's interested in Jake?" the anxious father asked, waiting for her to hand him a clean plate to dry.

"I promised not to say a word about it," Dora stated, her twinkling eyes giving his answer.

Don hugged his wife, soapy hands and all, and kissed her

smiling lips. "Wild horses couldn't drag it from you," he chuckled.

Derrick, older and wiser than his brother, dragged Dustin off to climb trees, leaving his sister and Jake in relative peace. François orbited Darlene, checking frequently to make sure she was still within easy reach.

Hands shoved into his trouser pockets, Jake strolled at Darlene's side, answering her spate of questions as well as he could. It was stimulating to interact on an equal level, no longer as adult and child, but as man and woman. Each was aware of the difference. Darlene was particularly uncertain, sometimes feeling bashful, other times plunging into deep waters with highly personal questions that might have offended a lesser man.

"I can't believe Mom never told me you were adopted," she told him. "Why didn't you tell me when you told her? Does it bother you?"

"Yeah, some," he answered honestly. "You have a family heritage to be proud of. Mine is less than optimum, to say the least. I accept my past, and I know that God allowed it for a purpose, but it still isn't what I would have chosen. I don't even know where my real mother is. She doesn't want me to know. That hurts."

Yes, there was pain in his eyes. Plenty of it. How could she ever have thought him invulnerable? "I. . .I guess it would hurt. I'm sorry, Jake. We won't talk about it if you don't want to." She wanted to touch his arm, but she didn't.

His shoulders lifted and fell. "There's no point in keeping secrets. I do know some things about my family, because my maternal grandmother visited me once at a foster home when I was nine, and I wrote down everything she told me. I never saw her again after the Edgewoods adopted me. Anyway, I am a true American, a Heinz fifty-seven, melting-pot original. Granny Devereaux was of Spanish and Cherokee extraction. Her husband, my grandfather, was Cajun. Granny told me that my father was Iranian, but I thought Mom said he was Armenian, so I'm not sure."

"It doesn't really matter. You are who you are, no matter where your ancestors came from. Now I know why you're always so brown. I feel like a ghost beside you." She stretched out her white arm beside his. It was strong and muscular for a woman's arm, but next to his arm it looked soft and dainty. She liked that effect.

He regarded their arms impassively without removing his hands from his pockets. "My mother is dark too. Her hair looked blue-black. She was beautiful at one time." He sighed.

"Did she have eyes like yours? Deep set, chocolate brown, with thick lashes."

"Is that what my eyes look like?" He paused, thinking. "Her eyes were brown, but not deep set like mine." He let his eyes rest on Darlene's face. "I prefer blue eyes, myself."

Feeling a tightening in her chest, Darlene blurted, "I'm looking forward to the squadron tour Tuesday. Can we really fly the simulator?"

Jake's lips twitched, but he accepted her lead. "Yes, but that's only for your family. I can't take the whole school group to the sim."

"What's it like being a Weapons System Officer? What exactly do you do?" She felt silly to ask such a question, but he didn't seem to mind.

"I work with the pilot to locate and attack targets. That's the simplified version. I can explain in more depth while we're in the simulator if you want me to."

"Are you good at it? At being a Wizzo?"

He looked into her wide eyes and smiled. "I think so. I wouldn't do it if I didn't think I was good at it."

"Do you plan to stay in the air force until you retire?"

"Not unless God wants me to."

"What will you do if you don't stay in?"

"Probably teach again. I'm still going to school to prepare

for that eventuality. I couldn't comfortably support a family on the wage I made as a high school teacher, so I'm hoping to teach at the college level." He turned off the main path, taking an overgrown trail through the gorse bushes.

Darlene hustled to catch up with him, tripping over a blackberry vine across her path. François pushed past her, his ears dangling gorse thorns and wild oat seeds. "You could at least say 'excuse me,' " she admonished the dog.

Under a huge oak tree she caught up to Jake, panting, "Are you working on your master's degree?"

He gazed into the spreading branches overhead, listening to a twittering bird. His voice was quiet. "I already have that. I'm working on a doctorate through Cambridge University. They've been considerate of my circumstances, that is, deployments and such."

Darlene's eyes boggled. "You're working on a doctorate? Why didn't you tell me?"

His eyes lowered to her flushed face. "You never asked."

"But. . .but I drone on and on about my classes and scholarships and future plans, and you only listen. Don't I bore you to death?"

He reached out to pull a gorse sticker from her hair. "Not at all."

"I can't believe how self-centered I am, Jake," she stated flatly. "I. . .I've talked to you for hours on end, yet I hardly know you. On the other hand, you know me nearly as well as I know myself—maybe better. I've told you things I haven't even told my mother! You know all my plans and dreams, my inmost thoughts. How can you bear me?"

"Only God knows your inmost thoughts, Darlene, and He loves you more than anyone else ever could." Jake's hands returned to his pockets, but his eyes made Darlene feel uncomfortable. He really did know her too well. "Do you know Him? I mean, do you know Him intimately, as your dearest, closest Friend?"

She frowned, taking a step back. "What do you mean?" She had wanted to talk with him about God, but she had planned to initiate the discussion.

His brows pulled together as he considered his reply. "I'm not sure how to put it. I've been concerned about you, but I don't want you to take this as a criticism. It's only that I. . ." He stopped, still searching for words. "I guess what I want to say is this: It's more important that you grow in knowledge of and love for Jesus than that you get to know Jake Edgewood. Only by learning to love and appreciate Him can any of us learn to fully love and appreciate one another."

Darlene stared, uncomprehending. "But I do love Jesus."

"I know you do. I'm not trying to offend you; I want to help."

"Why do you think I need help?" She sounded defensive.

"You're not content; you're still searching. I hurt when you hurt, so I'm recommending the cure that works for me. Growing up can be painful. I know; I'm still growing up spiritually, and I will be until the day I die."

Her resentment melted away, but she was still puzzled. "You seem spiritually mature to me."

He kicked at an exposed tree root. "Mature compared to whom? No one ever 'arrives' spiritually, Darlene. Only in heaven will we be made perfect, like Jesus. Always on earth we are growing into His likeness. It's a continuous process, and an often painful one. However, the pain of growth is infinitely better than the alternative of stagnation!"

His words made sense, but she was not prepared to analyze and assimilate them at the moment. She had often heard similar words from her parents, but they carried more weight when Jake repeated them.

Letting her eyes drift across the common, she spotted Derrick's red T-shirt. "The boys are at Piglet's House," their name for a hollow oak.

While following her conversational lead, Jake led her back

to the trail. "Derrick has sprouted up," he remarked.

"Yes," she regained animation. "He's as tall as I am, and he's only thirteen! He's dreadfully skinny, though. Like a twig."

"He looks a lot like I did at that age, but taller."

She trotted along beside him, trying to match his stride until snatching branches forced her to drop behind. "Were you really that skinny? You're not skinny now." Then she recalled her first impression of him. "Of course, you're not fat, your ribs even show, but you've got big muscles. . .I mean, at swim lessons Joanna used to call you a hunk, and I saw lots of other women watching. . ." Realizing that she was babbling, she broke off abruptly.

Jake halted in the middle of the trail and turned to stare at her. To her surprise, he looked more flustered than she did. His brown face had turned brick red. She couldn't determine whether he was pleased or irritated.

"Oh, Jake, I'm sorry! I know better than to make personal remarks, but I talk too much when I'm nervous. My tongue seems to run on its own, and I—"

To her utter confusion, he leaned over and lightly kissed her cheek.

"It's all right," he soothed. There was a new brightness in his face. "Never mind. We'll talk about something else. I have a surprise for you in my car, sort of a very late birthday gift." He took her hand and led her, unresisting, along the path.

"But. . .but you already sent me a card. You didn't need to get me a gift," she protested.

"Your birthday is only an excuse. I would have bought it for you anyway," he admitted. "I've had it for months."

"You could have mailed it to me."

He shook his head. "Nope. You'll see why not."

Arriving at Piglet's House, they had no further opportunity for private conversation. Jake climbed the tree with the boys, to Dustin's delight. Darlene watched Jake during the rest of their walk, admiring everything about him. Frequently she discovered him watching her, and she wondered what he was thinking. She still wore her peach knit top paired with blue jeans. Did he like it? Or was he only contemplating her spiritual condition?

Returning to the house, Darlene hung back until the boys had taken François inside, then begged, "May I open my present now?" Her eyes were glued to Jake's Cherokee. A box was visible through the rear window.

"Yup. Let's take it inside." He carried the cardboard box, not allowing her to touch anything, though she offered to carry the heavy plastic bag that came with it.

Darlene was too preoccupied to notice that the kitchen was empty. Jake noticed and mentally blessed Dora.

"All right, you may open it. Don't get your hopes up too high. It isn't diamonds or china." Now that the big moment had arrived, he feared she would be disappointed.

Darlene carefully lifted the flaps and stared at the wooden box inside. "What is it? It has pretty carving on it." She reached in to touch it.

"Here, I'll lift it out for you." A moment later he set the wooden box on the table. "Open it."

She obeyed. "Oh! It's a, uh, what-do-you-call-it. A record player."

"A gramophone. The records are in the bag." He watched her face doubtfully.

"How does it work?" She opened little doors in the front and turned the handle carefully.

"Pick out a record, and I'll show you."

A smile grew upon her face as she thumbed through the musty records. "Jake, these are great! How fun! I want to hear this one first." She handed it to him.

" 'Always,' by Irving Berlin," he read, then placed it on the felt-covered turntable. "First you wind up the handle until you feel resistance. Then you flip this switch, and when it's running at full speed you set the needle on the edge, like this. I bought you a supply of needles. It has two choices of volume. Open the front doors, and you have loud; close them, and you have soft."

A scratchy noise filled the room, then a strain of scratchy music.

Darlene beamed. "I love it! This is great! Just like out of an old movie." She quieted as a tenor voice began to sing "I'll Be Loving You Always."

Darlene joined in, but Jake did not know the words. He simply listened, drinking in her voice as she sang words he longed to hear.

Before the song ended, she was busily picking out her next selection. "How about 'Don't Fence Me In?' I haven't heard that for years."

"Whatever you like. . .Darlene." He had nearly added an endearment, but swallowed it. This day would be a memory to treasure, whatever the future might hold. He did not want to ruin it by moving too quickly and frightening her away.

Several songs later she was still listening with bright eyes, and he knew his gift had been a smashing success. "I adore 'Red Roses for a Blue Lady,' " she confided. "It's so sweet. I'm sure those roses 'did the trick' for him."

"I wasn't sure which records to buy, but I had heard of that song. Some of the others were shots in the dark, like 'What Are We Going to Do about Mary, the Poor Old Cow?' That one's in a class by itself." He leaned back in the kitchen chair, his legs straddling the table leg, his arms folded across his chest.

Darlene sat on the edge of a chair while each song played, then hopped up to change the records. She was aware that he watched her, and this knowledge heightened her enjoyment, coloring her cheeks and adding zest to her voice. She felt giddy, romantic, reckless. "I'm crazy about all of them!" she declared, hugging herself with delight. "Jake, this is the best present ever! How can I thank you?"

"I'll take a hug for starters," he joked, not really expecting her to take him seriously.

She came at him from the side, clasped his head to her breast, and tenderly kissed his forehead, whispering, "Thank you, dear, dearest Jake." Before he could react, he had been released.

Darlene spun away to change the record, concealing her glowing cheeks. Jake sat with open mouth, reliving that moment in his memory.

"Oooh, here's Nat King Cole!" she trilled. "Listen to this one, Jake." Her voice was too loud and cheerful, but neither of them noticed.

Swallowing hard, he sat back, but he didn't hear a note of "Too Young." Neither did Darlene. Avoiding each other's eyes, they sat like a pair of rocks until the song ended.

Jake checked his watch. "Time to get ready for evening service." He rose quickly, brushing his hands down his pant legs. "I'll, uh, go see what the boys are doing."

"I'll put the records away." As soon as he was out of the room, she dropped into his vacated chair and rested her forehead on her folded arms. "Oh, Josiah Kyle, I love you so much!" she squeaked.

fourteen

After church that evening Jake and Darlene took another walk on the common in the long summer twilight. They walked hand in hand without speaking, listening to birdsong, contemplating private thoughts. Darlene was deliciously aware that he might kiss her, and her body tingled in anticipation. His face was grave, as though serious thoughts preoccupied him, but she was too exuberant to care.

Beneath a spreading grove of oaks upon a slight rise, they stopped to look out over the common. Darlene felt Jake's grip on her hand tighten, and she turned to face him, her hopes written plainly on her face. He did not disappoint her. Still serious, he kissed her gently, tenderly. Darlene's passion flared like a bonfire, and she wrapped her arms around his neck, silently begging for another kiss, longing to be swept off her feet. He responded, kissing her with more intensity, then firmly pulled her arms from his neck. She heard him take a deep breath.

"What's wrong, Jake?" she murmured, leaning toward him. The only thing in life was her desire to be held and kissed by this man—this dear, beloved, wonderful man.

He could only shake his head, regret and wonder in his dark eyes. Still, he held her away, resisting her efforts to snuggle against him.

"Don't you want to kiss me anymore?" Doubt suddenly quenched her ardor. Perhaps her kisses affected him the way Rick's had affected her—not at all. What a dreadful thought! A new sympathy for Rick was born in her heart at that moment.

"Darlene," he began, his voice like gravel. Clearing his throat, he tried again. "Remember what you told me when I phoned on your birthday, how a romantic relationship needs to have commitment?"

She nodded, still puzzled. His hands on her wrists tightened, hurting her.

"Physical attraction isn't enough. I. . .I've been struggling with that for a long time now. It is important, yes, I've realized that, too, but it's not enough. There has to be more." It almost seemed as though he were talking to himself.

"What do you mean?" Darlene twisted her wrists to free herself. Was he telling her that he didn't love her? That he planned to marry that Teri woman?

He shook his head, trying to clear it. "There are too many barriers between us yet, Darlene. Until we can commit to one another we can't allow things to progress further. . ." his voice trailed away.

Anger swept over her. The perfect evening was spoiled beyond repair. "Right. Well, let's go home. There's a good movie on TV tonight." She stalked away, leaving him to follow at will.

❧

A group of women and children huddled together in the parking area of the squadron, waiting for stragglers. The wind, far too cold for a July morning, nipped at their faces. "Have you seen Jake?" Dora asked Betty Whitehead. "He promised to meet us out here at ten o'clock."

Betty shook her head. "Do you think we ought to go inside and ask?"

Joanna murmured to Darlene, "Jake is never late, and I can't believe he would forget about our tour."

Darlene wasn't sure what to say. How would Jake treat her today? What could she say to relieve the awkwardness? Was there still any hope for a future as Mrs. Josiah K. Edgewood?

At that moment a flight-suited figure emerged from the squadron door. "Here comes Peter Shackleton," Dora announced. "Maybe he knows where Jake is. Is anything wrong, Peter?"

Shackleton's expression lightened at sight of Dora's familiar, friendly face. "Hello, Dora. I have bad news and good news. At least, I hope it's good. Jake got pulled from this tour, but he asked me to cover for him, and I managed to reschedule myself long enough to escort you through most of your tour."

"I see. Thank you, Captain Shackleton. This is very kind of you!" She used his formal title for the benefit of the children. Beckoning to a quiet young mother, she gently pulled her forward to meet him. "Denise, this is Peter Shackleton, a friend from our church. Captain Shackleton, this is Denise Hooper, our group coordinator."

Peter shook hands with Mrs. Hooper, who said, "I believe everyone is here now. We're ready to begin the tour when you are."

The ladies shepherded their children into line, pairing them off for convenience' sake. High-school-age students hung loosely together off to one side; some of the girls helped herd the little ones.

Darlene was not satisfied with these arrangements. A squadron tour without Jake? Unthinkable! Was he doing this to punish her? She hurried to catch up with Shackleton as he opened the building's heavy front door. "But. . .but where is Jake?" Pairs of children filed past and lined up in the hallway.

Peter's narrow hazel eyes turned to her, expressing regret. "He was slated to fly, Darlene. I'm sorry."

Angry disappointment filled her. "You mean, he's going to miss the entire tour? But. . .but if you could reschedule yourself, why couldn't you reschedule him?"

Shackleton replied mildly, but the regret in his eyes dimmed. "A Wizzo was needed for this mission, and Jake's skills are in high demand. I am a pilot, not a Wizzo, therefore I could not take his place in the flight. I may be a sorry substitute here, but at least I'm qualified."

Darlene dropped her eyes. He was a poor target for her wrath. She felt foolish, but rather than back down she blundered on, "I know you carry lots of clout. It seems like you could have worked something out if you'd wanted to badly enough."

The last mother filed past them into the building. Shackleton gave Darlene only a fleeting glance. "I'm sorry you feel that way." He walked past her to begin the tour.

Avoiding her mother's eyes, Darlene followed the group around the squadron, then into the main briefing room, a small auditorium, where Shackleton showed them a slide presentation about McDonnell Douglas F-15E Strike Eagles, narrating it himself. During the question-and-answer session following, Darlene's thoughts wandered. Without putting her intentions into cogent thought, she determined to make Jake suffer for disappointing everyone this way. She almost resented her brothers for not appearing more disgruntled by the switch. They were asking questions and listening intently to Shackleton's answers.

"The step vans are waiting out front to drive you over to the hangar. Lieutenant Medwin will take over your tour from here. Thank you for being such good listeners." Shackleton handed over his microphone, then made his way down the aisle, waving good-bye to Darlene's brothers and a few other children he knew from church.

He paused beside Darlene's seat. "May I speak with you?"

With a sinking feeling in her stomach, Darlene followed him out to the hallway. She was as tall as he was, yet somehow she felt small in his presence, and she didn't like the sensation.

He turned to face her and spoke quietly. "I must apologize for being abrupt with you earlier. I was nearly as frustrated with the schedule changes as you were, but nowhere near as frustrated as Jake was. He's paying the price for being too good at his work. However, I do need to make it clear that, even if I could have pulled strings to keep him with you, I would not have done it. Important as your tour is to you, it is more important to the squadron to have our flight crews well trained. The mission must come first. This is a fact you had better accept quickly if you care for Jake."

Darlene was speechless. She nodded acceptance of his apology, knowing full well that she had been the one at fault. What did he mean by "if you care for Jake"?

"I hope you enjoy your sim flight this afternoon. I'm sure Jake'll be finished in time for that. Good morning." Peter nodded politely to her and walked away.

After a crowded ride to the flight line, the home-school group entered the huge cement hangar where their Eagle awaited. Darlene's eyes widened, her attention finally arrested. In the vast space of the hangar's interior, the jet appeared small at first. She had never before seen one up close, having never attended an air show.

Lieutenant Medwin gathered his audience in close, then began a walkaround of the jet, explaining each part and describing his job. Hoping he wouldn't recognize her, Darlene stayed in the back of the group. He probably wouldn't know her with her legs covered, anyway. She tried to listen, but much of his lecture was incomprehensible to her. Looking up at the jet's backseat beneath the raised canopy, she tried to picture Jake sitting there, but imagination failed her. She had seen him wearing his flight suit many times, but somehow it had never registered with her that he actually flew in these airplanes.

"Learning much?" A low voice buzzed against her ear, sending lightning chills up her spine.

"Ooh!" she gasped, sidling away before she realized the identity of the speaker. "Jake!" Spontaneous joy permeated her whispered cry.

He placed one finger over his smiling lips. "I can only stay a moment. Gotta go debrief. But I'll be with you at the simulator today, and for lunch. Twelve-thirty at the O'Club, right? I'll meet you in the lobby." He still wore his ejection-seat harness and carried his helmet bag in one hand. The outline of his oxygen mask was pressed into his face. Although his professional attire gave him an alien look, it was strangely reassuring to see him wearing glasses again.

"How. . .how was your flight?" she whispered.

He nodded. "Went well, considering that half my mind was here with you all." He gave her a wink. "Enjoy! See you later." He strode away.

A nudge from her mother brought Darlene to attention. "It isn't ladylike to stare!" Dora whispered. "You'll see him again in a few hours. What did Peter need to talk with you about earlier?"

"He explained that Jake's flight was more important than our tour."

Dora's brows knit. "That doesn't sound like Peter."

Darlene shrugged one shoulder. Thinking only of her eagerness to see Jake again, she tuned out the rest of the tour.

Jake met them at the Officers' Club at 12:30. "How did your tour go?" he asked, stuffing his flight cap into an ankle pocket. "Shack knows more than I do about the jet. I'm sure he gave a better tour than I could have done. I'll take you and Don around sometime and show you the flight planning room and the Panther Pub."

Except for a quick smile at Darlene, his attention was focused upon Dora, and he walked beside her into the club. Darlene followed behind with her brothers, coldness settling around her heart.

"We saw the pub," Derrick informed him. "Lieutenant Medwin took us through it after we saw the jet."

"Good. Sounds like the tour went pretty well. Do you think the other families liked it?" he asked, ushering them into the buffet line.

Dora picked up a tray and scanned the wall menu. "Very much. It was a huge hit—especially with the boys. We had a large turnout for a summer field trip."

"What did you think, Darlene?" Jake handed her a tray.

She shrugged, her expression freezing over as she renewed

her vow to make him pay. If he hadn't let her down, she wouldn't have made a fool of herself in front of Pete Shackleton. Shame for her own senseless behavior rankled—so she proceeded to make things worse. "It was all right." Nose slightly elevated, she turned her attention to the salad bar.

Jake's smile vanished.

Darlene was excruciatingly polite and proper throughout the meal, yet subtly made her displeasure known. It gave her a strange, malicious thrill to see the pain in Jake's eyes when she snubbed him. Dora tried to make up for her daughter's rudeness, but the effort made her voice slightly shrill, her laughter forced.

Jake dropped his napkin on his plate and checked his watch. "We'd better get over to the sim." He looked hopefully at Darlene. "Do you still want to see it?"

"Of course. You reserved it for us. I'd be rude to refuse." Her chin tilted ever so slightly.

Dora gave Jake a commiserating look, but she could do nothing to soften Darlene's blows. Jake had lost all desire to show Darlene the simulator, but he couldn't let Derrick and Dustin down. The boys were as enthusiastic as ever.

Darlene watched and listened in spite of herself as Jake explained the F-15E simulator to her brothers. The vast room with its network of computers was impressive, and the simulated cockpit snared her interest. A ledge ran around it, giving her plenty of room to stand and watch over Jake's shoulder as he explained how to take off, speaking through his headset to her brother in the front seat. Derrick was pilot for a day and loving it!

No longer would Darlene have trouble imagining Jake in the seat of a jet. He looked completely at home with the intricate controls. Her mind boggled when he described the myriad functions of each switch on the displays, and the radar system he worked with on a daily basis was far beyond her comprehension. Her disinterested mask slipped for the time being.

"Want to try flying it?" he offered without looking up.

She couldn't resist the lure. "All right."

He climbed out to stand beside her, then helped her climb in and fasten her seat belts. Leaning far over the side, he tried to help her set up her radar. "I guess you've got to be Wizzo, since Derrick won't hand over the stick."

"I'd rather be Wizzo, since that's what you do." She sounded like her usual sweet self, and Jake's spirits rose. Hanging farther over her than strictly necessary, he explained the computer system again, then ended up programming it himself.

She turned her head to ask a question and bumped her forehead against his smooth-shaven cheek. Warmth lapped over her. The question was forgotten.

"Ready to try? You need a chance to fly it yourself."

She snapped back to reality. "The stick keeps moving on its own."

"Derrick doesn't give up the ship easily." Jake moved to consult her pilot, then returned. "Now try it."

After several crashes, she managed to keep the jet airborne for three consecutive minutes. "I'm doing it!"

Jake grinned, eyeing her altitude indicator. "You're nearly in orbit, but that's better than being underground."

Her good mood lasted no longer than her turn in the simulator, to Jake's disappointment. She tore into Derrick for appropriating her spot at Jake's shoulder while Dustin sat in the front seat, then sulked when Jake took her brother's part. Abandoning the simulator, she walked over to the sim operator's station and began to quiz him about his job and the capabilities of the simulator. The young civilian contractor basked under her smile and warmed to his subject, forgetting to survey his computer monitors until Jake's irate voice over the radio recalled him to duty. Darlene suppressed a spiteful smile at the success of her ploy.

At least Derrick and Dustin had a fabulous day.

fifteen

Dora climbed into bed beside her husband. "Don, may I talk to you for a minute?"

Don laid down his book and opened his eyes. "Hmm?"

His wife chuckled. "How long have you been reading that page?"

"I have no idea what it says. Thanks for waking me up." He smiled sheepishly, stretched long arms over his head, and settled back with a deep sigh. "Now, what did you say?"

"I asked if I could talk to you about Darlene."

His thick brows lifted. "Is something wrong? I thought your tour today was a smashing success."

Dora sat cross-legged on the bed facing him and clutched her pillow in her lap. "It was, with everyone but Darlene. She was so unkind to Jake, as though it were his fault that he couldn't lead our tour!" Incredulity accented her voice. "I don't know what got into her, behaving that way! I felt like smacking her; not that it would have done any good. She was the picture of a spoiled brat, Don!"

"How did Jake react?"

"He looked hurt, but he was as sweet as ever. She thawed out a little while we were in the simulator, but afterwards she was worse than ever, flirting with the young man who operated the computers, or whoever he was. I wouldn't blame Jake if he washed his hands of her after that spectacle. I tried to confront her, but she wouldn't admit any fault."

"I did notice that she seemed withdrawn tonight. She hardly said a word at dinner." Don shook his head. "All these emotional upheavals aren't like our Darlene."

"Well, they're like the old Darlene, before Jake entered her life." Curling over the pillow, she studied her bare toes, speculating, "Do you think college did this to her?"

"I wonder if she's worrying about Teri," Don mused.

Dora shook her head in despair. "I have no idea. She doesn't want to talk with me today. After our wonderful talk the other night, I thought things would be great between us for a while. Do you want to try talking with her?"

Don looked startled. "Do you think I should?"

Dora met his gaze, and they stared at one another for a long moment. "I don't know, darling. I honestly don't know."

Don drew his lips in and out, twitching his mustache. "We need to pray for her."

"I pray for her every day." She looked almost affronted.

"No, I mean a special prayer session together, right now, just for Darlene. She needs our prayer support."

Dora nodded. "All right."

Together they knelt beside their bed, hand in hand, and prayed for their daughter according to the Spirit's leading.

❧

Darlene wanted to cry, but the ache in her heart was too deep for tears. Her face was scrubbed, her hair braided, her room straightened, her nightgown donned; there was nothing left to do but get into bed. Sitting on the edge of her bed, she scanned her bookshelves for a good novel, but none of them appealed. François leaped upon his folded blanket at the foot of her bed and curled up with a contented sigh. Darlene glared at him, resenting his peace of mind. Her feet twitched nervously. Her lips pressed into a hard line.

"I have every right to be angry," she whispered. All afternoon she had listed her grievances, dredging up slights, real and imaginary, some from years past, and tallying them on a mental slate. "I'm always nice, and I let people take advantage of me. I need to stand up for my rights once in a while. Let them all be shocked; they'll get over it."

This reasoning worked until she recalled Jake's sad face.

"I didn't just stand up for my rights; I walked all over him," she groaned, then stiffened, adding, "but he should have stood up for his rights and insisted upon leading our tour! He's too gentle and patient for his own good. And how dare he push me away when I tried to kiss him the other day! What kind of a man is he? He wants to control everything—well, he doesn't control me!"

Memory verses sneaked into her thoughts, "But the fruit of the Spirit is love, joy, peace, patience, kindness, goodness, faithfulness, gentleness, and self-control. Against such things there is no law."

Anger distorted her features. "It's not fair!" What, exactly, was not fair didn't matter at the moment. She was simply furious with Jake for demonstrating fruits that she was clearly lacking. Grabbing her Bible from her bedside table, she opened it to Galatians chapter five and read the entire passage, seething with resentment.

"What fruits did I demonstrate today?" she asked François with such vehemence that his ears flattened. "Here's a list: 'hatred, discord, jealousy, fits of rage, selfish ambition'." She snapped the book shut on her finger. "What a marital catch I am! The virtuous woman personified. After today, I'm sure Jake can't wait to pop the question—to somebody else!"

Bitter tears finally overflowed. "O God, sometimes I hate myself!" Burying her face in her pillow, she shook with wrenching sobs. François rose and poked his cold nose into her neck, offering comfort, but she was too miserable to even acknowledge him. He retreated and lay down again, blinking troubled brown eyes.

Darlene's thoughts raced, compiling a list of self-accusations that quickly outstripped her list of grievances against others. Discomforting revelations struck one after another: she had never really cared for Rick; she had only used him to feed her ego, to prove to the world that a popular boy could find her attractive, wishing only to see that affirming flare of admiration in his eyes whenever she felt low. Rick had been ready and willing to oblige her on every occasion, but when he attempted to satisfy the desires she had continually fanned into flame, she had self-righteously denounced him as a spiritually immature, designing male. How foolish she had been to entice a man that way!

That lesson yet unlearned, upon her return home she had tried the same trick on Jake, a mature Christian, with humiliating results, then proceeded to lose her temper with him when he attempted to curb her passionate advances.

Today everyone got an eyeful of the real me, Lord, the me You've seen all along, and they didn't like it. I'm selfish and mean and hateful and lustful and—well, You know what I'm like better than I do. I've been fooling myself along with everyone else. Please forgive me, and make me pure and truly sweet and good. I've tried so hard, but I can't change myself!

Still sniffing, she slowly sat up, blinking stinging eyes, and reached for a tissue. *I must write an apology to Rick first thing tomorrow morning, and apologize to Jake and to Peter Shackleton and to Mom and, oh, dear, a whole list of people!* It was a daunting prospect.

Opening her Bible randomly, she paged through Ephesians, reading bits and pieces as she went. Her attention was caught by Paul's directions to husbands and wives in chapter five, and for the first time she realized the significance of Christ's love for the church.

Jesus loves me with all the love I've dreamed of and longed for from a man! No man could ever possibly fulfill my fantasies, but He can and will. I've always loved Him, but my love has been shallow, almost like the affection I have for François. . .well, maybe deeper than that. More like my love for Grandpa. Real love, but distant. Pleasant, but not essential to my everyday life. I just take Him for granted. No excitement, no passion about it. But He wants, He deserves, much more than that from me.

Paging through the Scriptures, she soaked up verses with relish, reading them with new understanding and appreciation. At last, she began to comprehend Paul's longing to depart this life and be with Christ, a longing she had always thought strange. Each reference to Jesus' love brought warmth to her heart, and she devoured each mention and description of Him like a lover reading news of her beloved. That thought lifted her eyes from the page, and her lips formed an O.

So this is what Mom means when she says I lack depth of love for Jesus! I thought she was being silly when she talked about "falling in love with Jesus," but that is exactly how I feel—in love. And His love is forever. I don't need to wonder whether or not He loves me; I don't need to worry that He loves another girl better; He'll never leave me for any reason; He'll never be shocked or disillusioned by my sinfulness 'cause He knows the worst about me already! The only problem is. . .

Lying back on her pillow, she felt guilty for even letting herself think that God's love might be lacking in any way, but the thought persisted. *Lord, I know Your love is all-sufficient, but . . .well, Your arms are around me, I know, but I can't feel them, and sometimes I feel so alone. Would You, could You, let me feel them somehow? This is a silly request, but You know all about my silliness and love me anyway, so I'm daring to ask.*

Placing her Bible on the bedside table, she reached over to turn out her light, humming the old hymns, "Leaning, leaning, leaning on the Everlasting Arms. . . ," then, "There is a place of quiet rest Near to the Heart of God." Resting in the darkness, she closed her eyes, thinking about Jesus, reveling in His love for her. As she lay there, warmth enveloped her, a sense of security and belonging such as she had never known before. He was with her, holding her, treasuring her, loving her with a love beyond dreams.

Tears trickled down her temples, and her lips trembled with joy. "O Jesus! You are all I need! I feel Your arms. I really do!"

sixteen

Jake lifted his head when he heard a familiar whistle outside his office door. Sure enough, a moment later Peter Shackleton passed by, caught sight of him, and doubled back. "What are you doing here so late? Thought you were on leave."

"Not till tomorrow. I've got to get this file up-to-date before I leave tonight. Haven't had a chance until now."

"You've been working like a dog this week. Guess you know you'll be missed around here next week, eh?" Shack leaned one shoulder against the weapons shop door frame.

"What an honor!" Jake rolled his eyes. "One slave gone makes more work for the others." Then he sniffed. "I shouldn't complain, but the negative attitude is contagious."

Shack nodded. "That I know. Keep the faith, bud. Gotta head out; Polly's keeping dinner for me. Have a good vacation. You've got family coming, right?"

"My sister and brother-in-law, and his sister. I'm picking them up in the morning."

"Oh, that's right, the old flame cometh to rekindle the fire. Gonna bring them to church Sunday?"

Jake smiled acknowledgement of Peter's teasing. "Sure. I'll introduce you."

Peter gave him a considering look. "I'm sure your sister will want to meet Darlene."

Jake rubbed his forehead, dropping his eyes to the papers on his desk. "I hope so."

"You know, your girl called me at home the other day to apologize for her attitude the day of the squadron tour. Do you think her parents prompted that, or did she do it on her own? She sounded sincere."

"She's too old for Don and Dora to order around. It must have been her own idea. Why? Was she rude to you too?"

"Don't worry about it. I won't hold it against her. I know what my woman gets like when things don't go her way, and Darlene isn't as mature as Polly is. Have you talked with her since Tuesday?"

"No, but I've hardly been home. I was supervisor of flying yesterday, and I flew twice today. She might have tried and couldn't get me."

"You need an answering machine."

"Maybe so." He checked his watch, and his shoulders drooped. "It's too late to call tonight, and I'm heading to the airport first thing in the morning."

Peter walked in to lean both hands on the desk. "Let God handle it, Jake. He can and will."

"She's so young, Shack. I'm beginning to wonder if I'm wrong about it being God's will. . ." He ran out of words.

Peter examined his face. "You're losing patience?"

Jake's shoulders slumped further. "She'll be going back to college in a few weeks. You know my assignment here at the 'Heath ends in January, and who knows where in the world I'll be stationed next? Time seems to be running out on me, but I can't rush her into growing up. She's the woman I want to marry, but I want her now, not several years hence after years apart. It seems like my chances are slipping away, and I can't do anything about it."

Peter thought deeply as he regarded Jake's pained expression. "Isn't her college near Raleigh, North Carolina? Have you thought about asking for an assignment at Seymour Johnson Air Force Base? It's near Raleigh."

Jake's shoulders straightened, his eyes widened. "I hadn't thought of that, Shack. I can't believe I never even thought about that!"

"You're welcome." Peter gave a mock salute and turned away.

੩ఎ

At 5:00 A.M. Friday, Jake pulled up in front of the Althorps' house. He knocked softly on the front door, hoping François wouldn't bark and wake the entire family. To his surprise, Darlene opened the door, a wagging poodle at her feet. "Derrick overslept, Jake. He's getting dressed. Here are the keys to the van. Want to come in?"

"Uh, just a minute. I'll start the van and let it warm up." Hurrying away, he shook his head, trying to clear it. Darlene looked cuddly and sweet in that eyelet robe, with her sleep-smudged face, tousled hair, and bare pink toes.

Back in the entryway, leaving the door ajar, he allowed himself the pleasure of looking, but not touching. Her pale cheeks crimsoned. "I know I look awful, but you don't have to stare! I want to say something quickly before Derrick comes down. I've tried to call you several times, but you're never home."

"I've been working crazy hours. You don't look awful—" he began, but she cut in.

"No woman looks good first thing in the morning. I bet even Polly Shackleton looks ragged at this hour. Anyway, I want to tell you how sorry I am for the nasty way I treated you the other day. All I can say is, I was being selfish, hateful, and made everyone miserable, and I am terribly sorry. Will you forgive me? You were right, Jake, I don't know God very well, and I wasn't willing to get to know Him better because I was afraid it might not be comfortable. It isn't comfortable to admit my sinfulness and apologize like this, but I know it's what God wants me to do, and Jesus is worth it! He has already forgiven me." Her eyes glowed in spite of the hour. "I'm finally learning what it means to love and be loved!"

Jake blinked. Her flood of words took a moment to sink in. Then a smile transformed his face. "I can't tell you how happy I am to hear it. I've been praying for you for a long time, and I know your parents have been too."

Derrick staggered down the stairs. "I'm ready. Sorry, Jake. My alarm didn't go off. If Darlene hadn't set her alarm, I'd still be sawing logs." He thrust his arms into a jacket.

Jake thumped the boy's shoulder. "Sisters do come in handy, after all. Bring something to eat. It's a long drive."

Derrick headed toward the kitchen; Darlene followed Jake to the front door. "Drive carefully."

"I will. Maybe I'll see you when I bring Derrick and the van back. Tell your folks thanks for loaning them both." Jake turned at the door and reached out a hand. "And I forgive you; I always will," he whispered.

She took his hand in both of hers. "Thank you, Jake."

Derrick pushed between them, disrupting the tender moment. "'Scuse me," he mumbled around half a bagel.

Jake followed him, giving Darlene a little wave. "See you later," he murmured, reluctant to leave.

"Bye!" She waved until the van disappeared around the corner. Turning back to the stairs, she contemplated the look in Jake's eyes. Physical attraction wasn't enough, he had said. Had he been speaking for himself, or for her? Was it love he felt for her, or did he only consider her a friend and spiritual protegé? Had he kissed her because she had seemed to expect it and invite it, or because she attracted him? Confused, she could only shake her head.

Darlene ended up being out when Jake returned, so she grilled Derrick that evening, sitting across from him at the dining table. "What are they like? Did Jake seem happy to see them?"

Dora bluntly asked the question Darlene couldn't put into words. "How did he greet Teri?"

Derrick chewed a bite of blackberry pie before answering. "He hugged her. He hugged all of them. It looked like they were happy to be together. They're nice people."

Dora and Darlene exchanged frustrated glances. His mother persisted. "I mean, was it romantic?"

The boy gave her a tolerant smile. "Nobody did any mushy kissing, though that Teri lady did hang on Jake's neck for a while, and I don't think she would have minded a kiss."

Darlene's heart started beating again.

"Aren't they coming for dinner Sunday? You can see for yourselves then. Whew! I feel like I'm being interviewed for a tabloid," Derrick complained to his father.

Don tried to disguise his chuckle as a cough, but earned a guilty glare from his wife. He pushed his empty dessert plate away and sat back. "He's right, Dorie. Have patience."

It wasn't easy, but Dora and Darlene curbed their curiosity until Sunday. The frenzy of preparation before church that morning amused Don further. "Smells good in here," he remarked, wandering into the kitchen. "Can I help?"

"Yes, you can get cereal and bowls out for yourself and the boys," Dora instructed. "We're almost ready, I think. Darlene, we'll let the dough rise during church and pop the rolls into the oven when we get home. It isn't the proper length of time, but I don't think it'll hurt. Go ahead and finish getting ready, honey."

After Darlene left, Dora stood contemplating for a moment. "Now, we've got the ham in the oven, the green bean casserole and candied yams ready to bake, the pies for dessert—oh! We need ice cream! Would you stop at the Four Seasons and buy some for us after church, Don? Oh, and I need to iron the tablecloth."

Brawny arms folded across his chest, Don leaned his hips against the counter and watched his wife bustle past. He snatched her apron string, and her momentum untied the bow. "I saw Gary Cooper do that in a movie once. It really works."

Catching her falling apron, Dora turned to berate him, then melted and gave him a hug. "I'm being silly, aren't I?" she murmured against his shirtfront.

"Yes, but I'll enjoy the good food. Relax and enjoy, sweetheart. Remember the real reason for your hospitality: to show love to brothers and sisters in Christ. You're not out to impress."

She nodded, "Darlene is being a better example of love and peace than I am, and she's the one facing possible competition."

"She's been a different girl these last few days. Guess our prayer session worked." Don rested his chin on top of his wife's head and rubbed her back.

"I wondered if the change would last, but it's been several days now, and she's risen to every challenge with flying colors. Even Derrick and Dustin have noticed the difference."

"God doesn't do things halfway." Don looked down into his wife's face. "You sure look pretty today."

Slightly rattled, Dora fluttered her eyes and pulled away. "Don, don't get me distracted! We're leaving for church in just a few minutes, and you haven't eaten breakfast yet."

ঽ

Don looked out across the congregation, noting a few new faces, missing a few regulars. Several church members were on holiday. He tried not to stare at the three visitors with Jake Edgewood, stealing only quick glances at them during the hymns.

Dora felt more free to stare, hidden as she was by the piano. During the announcements, she inspected them carefully. The slender young man with the reddish-blond beard had a nice face. The woman he shared a hymnbook with must be his wife, Leigh, Jake's adopted sister. Leigh Sutton was angular and pale, but she dressed well, playing up her best features. Her sweet expression more than compensated for her lack of beauty. She leaned against her husband, Reg, gazing up at him with adoring eyes.

Jake shared his hymnbook with the other woman. Dora found herself looking for Teri's weaknesses, and dropped her eyes to her hands on the keyboard. *Lord, help me to love this girl as You do. Let me see Teri Sutton through Your eyes of love.*

It was time for another song, so Dora had no chance to examine Teri. After the song she took her seat between Dustin and Don. Jake was watching her from across the aisle. A knowing smile curled his lips. With a clear conscience, Dora winked at him and gave a little nod, then turned her attention to the sermon.

Darlene sat with her usual group of friends, doing her best to behave normally, making frequent silent pleas for help. She felt God's presence sustaining her, enabling her to reply gently to the verbal jabs aimed by her friends. Everyone took it for granted that she would be jealous of Jake's lady friend, and they were evidently surprised by her peaceful demeanor. She took only two or three quick glances at Jake's companions, enough to see that Teri was a pleasant-looking woman, but no beauty.

Lord, am I wrong to even think a thing like that? Beauty is in the eye of the beholder, and perhaps Jake finds her attractive because of her gentle, quiet spirit. He's the type of man who looks for inner beauty, and I'm afraid she'll have the edge on me there since I waited so long to let You give me a makeover. That idea brought a smile to her face. *A spiritual makeover, that's what I'm having.*

She glanced back at Teri's round face, realizing that the other woman could end up becoming a close friend of the Althorp family if she were to marry Jake and stay in England. Steeling herself, Darlene tried to imagine visiting Teri and Jake at their future home in a nearby cottage. Pain laced through her heart. *Lord, You'd better work faster on this makeover. I'm still selfish and dreadfully jealous!*

Setting her mind on the sermon, Darlene managed to glean encouragement from the Scriptures. She was thankful for the distraction and praised her Lord continually for providing the strength she needed to meet this day.

Lord, help me to be Your humble servant, willing to remain in the background and give of myself. Empty me of all but love—Your giving love, not my demanding love.

Dora's dinner was delicious, by unanimous vote, and the

conversation around the extended table that afternoon was stimulating, encouraging, and satisfying to all—or nearly all. Jake noticed Darlene's reluctance to push herself forward. His attempts to draw her into conversation were largely unsuccessful, though she answered his questions politely and listened to the others speak with genuine interest.

Teri told about her work at a home for mentally disabled children; Leigh described her job as a court reporter; Reg told some amusing stories about his experiences working as supervisor of a major shopping mall. All of them shared anecdotes about Jake's past, some of which he would have preferred to keep secret. Dora amused the guests with her attempts to guess Jake's name. She had recently purchased a book of names, and was working her way through the *Js*.

After dinner, Darlene cleared the table and washed dishes while the others gravitated out to the backyard, setting up lawn chairs on the cement deck and enjoying the fine afternoon. She could hear their voices through the open window above the kitchen sink, though their words could not be distinguished. To keep herself company, she began to softly sing one of the hymns from church that morning, "Great Is Thy Faithfulness." Absorbed in her music, she didn't hear the door creak open.

"Need help?"

Darlene spun around, spattering the floor with suds. Teri stood behind her. "Oh, you startled me!"

"Sorry. I wasn't trying to sneak up on you. I was listening to your singing. You have a gorgeous voice." It was an honest compliment, given with a smile.

Darlene smiled back. "Thank you. Do you sing?"

Teri nodded. "I'm no soloist, but I can carry a tune. Here, let me dry those for you." She picked up a towel and started on the plates. "Do you know 'Until Then?' That's one of my favorites."

Song after song poured from their hearts as they worked

side by side. Teri's tentative soprano was strengthened by Darlene's rich harmony. Occasionally their glances caught and they shared a smile. When the last pan had been dried and put away, Teri gave Darlene a hug. The top of her head barely reached Darlene's shoulder. "You're the dearest thing! No wonder Jake enjoys spending time with this family; I've never known nicer, more loving people anywhere! You're so glamorous and beautiful that I was prepared to dislike you, but I can't."

The frank compliment took Darlene by surprise. Glamorous? Beautiful? "I'm not really nice and loving, Teri. It's Jesus in me."

Teri nodded. "That's true of any of us, Darlene. The real test comes when things don't go our way." Her gray eyes held a message, but Darlene did not understand. "I have a tendency to boss people around, and I frequently find myself telling God what He should do. It's not easy to find out that my plans are not God's plans."

"No, it wouldn't be," Darlene agreed.

Her puzzled eyes told Teri that she needed to speak plainly. "I came to England intending to convince Jake to marry me. We've always loved each other, so I thought our eventual marriage was a foregone conclusion. I thought he was merely exercising self-control when he refrained from any physical expression of love. Now I know it was because kissing me never even occurred to him. He doesn't love me that way; he never has."

Teri's sad eyes caught at Darlene's heart. "Oh, Teri!" She could imagine how such rejection would hurt. "Are you certain? I mean, you've only been here two days. Maybe in time—"

"I could tell the moment I got off the plane, Darlene. He was no happier to see me than he was to see Leigh and Reg. He tried to explain in a letter several months ago, but I thought it was only because we had been apart for so long. I didn't understand about you."

"About. . .about me?"

Teri sighed. "I hope and pray that someday a man will look at me the way Jake looks at you, my dear. He's so smitten, it almost hurts to watch him. He told Leigh that he's trying to be patient and give you time to grow up, but it isn't easy for him. He'd marry you now if he could."

Darlene could scarcely breathe. "He said that?"

"Yes. He also told us that he's asked for an assignment at a base near your college. His assignment here ends in January."

"Why hasn't he said anything to me?"

"He will, I'm sure. He doesn't want to complicate your life right now. You received a full scholarship for next school year, right?"

"Yes, I did, but I'd give it up in a heartbeat rather than lose Jake!" Darlene declared.

"Maybe so, but I don't think he'd feel right to ask that of you. What's your major, Darlene?"

"I haven't declared one yet, if you must know. I can't decide, so I'm taking mostly Bible classes and the basics."

"Where does this pitcher go?" Teri held up Dora's crystal pitcher.

"Here, I'll put it away. It goes on the top shelf."

The kitchen door swung open to admit Jake. "Hate to interrupt, but I came in to ask if you two wanted to take a walk on the common. Everyone else is going."

Darlene and Teri exchanged glances, both feeling thankful he hadn't come a few minutes sooner. "Sure," Teri replied. "We're finished in here." She headed for the door.

"Thanks for your help, Teri."

Teri caught the double meaning and flashed Darlene a smile. "Anytime, honey. That's what sisters are for." She stopped in front of Jake. "Excuse me, please, Josey."

He frowned, but couldn't keep an indulgent smile from his eyes. "Don't call me Josey, and there's no excuse for you."

He stepped aside.

Teri playfully punched at his stomach. "Thanks, Josey. I'll be ready for the walk in a minute; just let me duck into the bathroom." No one saw or suspected the tears she dabbed away in a private moment, no one except a loving Father in heaven. Teri had long ago learned to lean on Him for the strength she lacked.

"Could you hear our impromptu concert from out there?" Darlene asked, wiping off the countertop.

Jake leaned against the doorpost, hands in his trouser pockets. "Yes, we thoroughly enjoyed it; wondered if you'd take requests. I'm glad you've made friends with Teri. She's like a sister to me."

Turning, Darlene regarded him openly, trying to comprehend what Teri had told her. *This man wants to marry me! Has wanted to marry me for a long time!* Jake had removed his suit coat and tie and rolled up his sleeves. The white broadcloth shirt made his face and arms seem browner, his eyes darker than ever. Familiar and beloved though he was, the thought of marrying him was suddenly rather frightening. *How well do I really know him?* Her hands fluttered as she draped the dishrag over the faucet and rubbed her damp palms down her sides. *Am I ready for all that marriage means?*

"Darlene? Are you all right? You've been unusually quiet today." He approached her hesitantly, seeming to sense her ambivalent feelings.

"I. . .I'm all right. I like Teri a lot, and your family. Have you been enjoying their visit?" She tried to speak normally, but sounded breathless. Wild thoughts flashed through her mind. Remembering Rick's attempts to make love to her, she wondered what it would be like to have Jake desire her in that way. The mere idea was enough to set a fire burning within her. Did he desire her? It was her fondest wish come true, and yet, unlike wishes, reality could be alarming. How should she act? What should she say? Old, familiar Jake, her dear friend and companion, suddenly seemed like a mysterious stranger.

"Very much. I wanted to ask if you could join us for a few sight-seeing trips this week. Leigh would like to get to know you while she's here."

Darlene gripped the countertop behind her with both hands, struggling to breathe normally. "I don't know," she stalled. "I. . .I've made plans. . .promised Polly I'd baby-sit."

His brows contracted as he tried unsuccessfully to read her mind. "Every day?"

"No, but. . .I'm not sure when." She knew she was being unreasonable, but couldn't seem to help herself. The sudden onslaught of conflicting emotions was more than she could handle. *Lord, help me! I've lost control again!*

"Are you two coming?" Reg stuck his head through the doorway behind Jake. "We're ready to head out."

Darlene hurried to don her shoes, grateful for the reprieve. Jake followed her, determination to root out her problem putting a line between his brows. A few minutes in the company of her family snapped Darlene back to reality, and she did her best to be a good hostess for the rest of the day. Jake watched her closely and was relieved to see her at least outwardly back to normal. She made an effort to talk with Leigh, joked with Teri, and charmed Reg with her smiles. Jake decided to leave well enough alone.

They saw little of each other that week. Jake was busy escorting his guests around East Anglia; Darlene kept herself occupied with work and with sewing a fall wardrobe. She was relieved that he didn't ask her to join his "tour group" again, yet another part of her was piqued that he had given up the idea so easily.

Every time she thought of him or caught sight of him that week her blood ran hot. Memories of intimate glances and the touch of his lips against hers flashed through her mind, bringing color to her cheeks and a glow to her heart. "He loves me!" she informed François several times each day. Somehow, expressing it to her faithful listener made Jake's love seem more real.

seventeen

At last Friday came, and Jake's guests boarded a train for Scotland. When Darlene returned home from cleaning Mrs. Whitman's house, he was waiting for her in the family room, engrossed in a game of checkers with Dustin. He rose when she entered, bumped the board with his leg, and sent the players flying.

"I win by default," Dustin claimed in disgust, scooping up his checkers.

"Hello, Jake. Get your family off all right?"

"Yes, and I've got the rest of the day free. Would you. . .do you want to go on an outing? Just the two of us? I thought maybe we could drive up to Sandringham House or Castle Rising." He was dressed like a beach bum: blue tank top, denim shorts, sandals. Perfect attire for a hot summer day.

Darlene glanced down at herself. "It sounds fun, but give me a minute to clean up. I'll be right down." She grinned on her way upstairs. One glance at his strained, hopeful face had answered many of her doubts.

Jake sat down, still flustered, and helped Dustin gather the pieces. "Sorry about that."

"Why don't you two just get married and settle down?" Dustin griped. "Things would be a lot more peaceful around here."

Jake dropped a piece he had just picked up, unable to control his shaking hands. This was the day; he was going to tell her today. How would he survive until then?

Dustin easily won the next game, for Jake paid little attention to strategy. Darlene returned, showered and dressed in a blue tank top, denim shorts, and sandals. Her clothes matched

Jake's; she hoped he would notice, but doubted it.

Jake stood up again, forgetting that Dustin existed. "Ready?"

"Yes, but I need to let Mom know where we're going. When do you think we'll be home?"

"It might be late. I thought maybe we could go to dinner or walk on the beach or something." Darlene's fine brows lifted, and Jake felt his face grow hot. "If. . .if that's all right with you."

"Sure, it is." She disappeared into the kitchen for a few minutes, and came out with her own cheeks glowing. "She said that would be fine."

Jake handed her into his Jeep as though she were made of spun glass. Darlene felt giddy when he climbed in beside her. Her entire body tingled with anticipation. Something exciting would happen today!

They spoke of inconsequential things during the drive north. Jake told her about their sight-seeing trips that week, and Darlene told him about her baby-sitting adventures. It might have been boring conversation except that the company made anything interesting. Darlene was surprised when road signs indicated they were nearing Sandringham House.

"Have you been here before?" he asked, turning into the wide drive of the queen's house.

"No, I haven't. We tried to come once, but the queen was in residence at the time, so we couldn't tour the house." Darlene looked about at the expansive grounds. "What beautiful gardens!"

"Yeah, I thought this might be worth seeing."

Jake held her hand as they strolled through the open rooms of the palace among the summer crowds. He bought her a guidebook to the house, and she couldn't help thinking that it was a good thing, for she surely wouldn't remember anything about the place without that book to remind her; she was too caught up in Jake to notice mundane things like gold-plated dishes and priceless tapestries.

They wandered through the gardens, alone, yet surrounded by people. At the gift shop, Jake bought a china plate with a painting of the palace for Darlene and a leather bookmark for himself. "To remember it by," he told her with a hesitant smile. She couldn't help thinking that she could have been reminded by something much less expensive, but never in the world would she say so!

Hugging her gift to her chest, she thanked him with all her heart. "This will be a lifelong treasure, Jake."

"I hope so." He glanced at her with a puzzlingly sheepish expression. She couldn't understand why he would feel shy; she had given him every encouragement. It was totally unlike Jake to be bashful.

They dined in a small, obscure pub in Sandringham village, with the proprietor's obese Labrador retriever begging beside their table. It was a quiet meal; Darlene often felt Jake's gaze, but his eyes always dropped when she looked up. She had more luck conversing with the dog than with him.

The sun was dropping rapidly toward the horizon when they left the Hunter's Rest. "Now where?" Darlene inquired. "Do we have to go home yet?"

"Not if you don't want to. There's a nice beach near here. Want to go for a walk on the sand?"

"Yes!" No hesitation in that reply. Maybe he would open up to her during a long walk. It couldn't hurt to try.

During the short drive, Darlene frequently glanced at Jake's profile and told herself, *he wants to marry me. He's been waiting for me to grow up, and he loves me.* Somehow it was difficult to believe tonight.

At the beach, Jake helped Darlene out of the car and took her hand in a firm grasp. The parking area held few cars, for the sun had dropped low in the sky, withdrawing its summer heat. The tide was in, covering all but a narrow strip of sand. Only a few die-hard beachcombers remained.

"Let me take my sandals off," Darlene begged, pulling her

hand out of his grasp. Jake followed her example, and they strolled along the waterline, swinging their sandals, wet sand clinging to their feet.

"Jake, is something wrong? You've been acting strangely all day."

"Have I?" He gave her another of those sideward glances.

She stopped, irritated, and placed both fists on her hips. "Yes, you certainly have. What's with you?"

He sighed. "I don't know. Guess I'm nervous. You've been. . .different lately too. Sometimes I've felt like you're afraid of me."

She blushed and covered her hot cheeks with both hands; her sandals spattered sand in every direction "I know. . . I. . .I don't even understand myself."

"You don't have to be afraid of me, Darlene," he said softly.

She nodded, then blurted, "You don't have to be afraid of me either."

He blinked. "Don't I? You're pretty scary sometimes, kiddo."

"Only at five in the morning or when I don't get my way."

The gentle teasing relaxed them both. Jake glanced around, spied a jumble of large rocks nearby, and led her to them. "Should have thought to bring a blanket along to sit on," he mused, settling with his back against the largest rock.

"I should have thought to bring a sweater," Darlene added, dropping beside him. The twilight was quickly fading, and the sea breeze had a sharp bite.

"Cold?" He lifted one arm invitingly, and she finally got her wish: to snuggle against his side and wrap her arms around his body. It felt every bit as wonderful as she had imagined. The sand was chilly beneath her, but he was warm and solid. His other arm came around her, pulling her even closer, and for a while they simply sat there, afraid to move or speak lest the moment end.

Darlene's arm, the one behind his back, went numb, but she ignored it. Jake's heart thumped beneath her cheek; his breath stirred her hair. He felt tense. His fingers began to caress her bare arm, then rub her back.

"Darlene?"

She lifted her head, slid one hand up to turn his face toward hers, and kissed him, thrilling to his response. One kiss led to another, and for several minutes they were lost in pleasure, giving way to their rising passions. Then Darlene felt him pause, his face buried in her neck, and regather his self-control. Slowly he lifted his head, letting his cheek rub against hers, gave her lips a parting kiss, and leaned back against the rock. "Enough, sweetheart."

Although thankful for his respect and restraint, she also wished he wouldn't stop. "Just a little more?"

He smiled and shook his head. "Thought you said I didn't need to be afraid of you?"

She pouted smilingly and leaned against the rock beside him, no longer feeling cold. "Am I dangerous?"

"Potentially lethal. My only defense is. . ." He sat up, resting his elbows on upraised knees.

"What?" she prompted.

"I. . .um, I've been meaning to tell you that I've asked to be stationed at a base near your college starting in January."

"Teri told me."

"She did? Why that little traitor. . .what else did she tell you?"

"Oh, some interesting things." Darlene ran her fingers across his chest, admiring the way the knit clung to his swimmer's muscles. "Like why you asked to be stationed near me."

He grabbed her hand, only to press it to his heart. "And. . . what did you think?" He strove to read her expression in the darkness, but could only see the whiteness of her smile.

"I was surprised, but I rather liked the idea."

"Did you? Darlene, we're talking marriage, you know. Lifetime, until death do us part. To love, honor, and cherish. Keeping to me only. Are you sure about this?"

She rubbed her cheek against his smooth shoulder. "Completely sure. I've had a few days to think about it and adjust to the idea, and I can't think of anything I'd like better than to be your wife for the rest of my life, Josiah Kyle. You're my best friend, my favorite person in the whole world, and you keep me in line even better than my parents can. The more I grow to love Jesus, the more I grow to love you, maybe because I see so much of Him in you."

He rested his chin on top of her head and closed his eyes in silent thanksgiving. "So maybe Teri did me a favor, breaking the idea to you early."

"Maybe she did. I don't know why you'd want to marry a silly girl like me, but I'm not going to talk you out of it. When can we get married?"

"Well, your dad suggested during your Christmas break. I'll have several weeks of leave between assignments, and we could spend the time taking a honeymoon and setting up house."

Darlene sat up. "My dad suggested it? You mean, you've already discussed all this with my parents?"

"I had to ask their permission before I asked you, Darlene. You're very young yet, you know."

She grimaced, but accepted the truth. "I guess so. It just doesn't seem very romantic."

"There's one hitch to all this: I might not get the assignment I asked for."

"Then what would happen?"

"I don't know. We'll have to cross that bridge if we come to it."

"I would marry you anyway, Jake. You're more important than a scholarship."

He hugged her gently. "Thank you, sweetie. It means a lot

to hear you say that. Now, we need to get home and talk this over with your folks."

"Yes, husband-to-be. When do I get my ring?"

He rose and hauled her to her feet for a quick kiss. "Mercenary woman. We'll pick it out ASAP, all right?"

&

To Darlene's shock, her parents had different ideas. Neither of them thought the engagement should be official until after Jake's assignment came through.

"It's only money, yes, but you earned the scholarship, Darlene, and it would be poor stewardship to throw it away. Your wedding could wait until next summer," Don explained. "It wouldn't hurt either of you to wait a few more months."

The young people accepted this as well as could be expected, though Darlene shed many tears. "This means we have to part in a few weeks with nothing definite between us," she moaned dismally. "And how long will it be before we find out? It could be months!"

"Probably will be," Jake admitted, "but I understand how you feel about this, Don and Dora."

His mature acceptance of her parents' decision set poorly with Darlene. She was about to blow up when a small voice within reminded her, *patience is a fruit of the Spirit, Darlene. Are you demonstrating it? And how about respect for your parents and submission to their authority? How can you expect to be a submissive wife in a few months if you won't be a submissive child now?*

"All right," she gave in. "We'll wait."

eighteen

Darlene pulled into the driveway and parked. Yes, this must be the place; that flower wreath on the front door looked like Polly's decorating taste. What a lovely home Peter and Polly had here in North Carolina! Easily twice the size of the cottage they had rented in England.

Polly opened the front door as Darlene climbed out of her borrowed car. "Hello! You made it!" The two women exchanged fond hugs. "Oh, Darlene, it's so good to see you again, and it seems so strange to have you here in Goldsboro. Strange but very, very nice. I've missed you and your mom a lot. Here, let me help you with your bags."

"I only have this one overnight case, Polly, but thanks. You and Peter are so good to let me stay with you this weekend—"

"Nonsense! It's our pleasure entirely. We wanted to have Jake stay here, too, but he thought it best to stay in the motel with the other crews. He's probably right. Pete said he'd call when the Lakenheath jets land; he expected them around four o'clock or so."

"I wanted to go watch them land, but Jake said he'd rather meet me here." Darlene sounded wistful. "He called yesterday to make sure I was still coming."

Polly held open the screen door for her friend, smiling knowingly, then led the way upstairs. "After a ten-hour flight across the Atlantic, he won't feel fit to be seen until he showers. From what Peter says, the guys look, smell, and feel like something that crawled out of a sewer by the time they land. He doesn't want you to see him that way.

"Here's your room, and the bathroom is around the corner here."

"Thank you, Polly. This is beautiful! I'd forgotten how big American houses are." She dropped her case on the foot of the bed and gazed around the room in admiration.

Polly chuckled. "Yes, and there are screens on the windows, mixer faucets, closets, and untold other modern wonders."

"Where is Drew?" Darlene glanced around, finally noting the baby's absence.

"He's asleep. He'll be excited to see you."

"I wonder if he'll remember me. Probably not."

"Oh, I wouldn't be surprised if he did. He adored you last summer. Now I need to get started on dinner. Come keep me company while I work?"

"I'd rather keep you company while we work. Please don't make me be a spectator."

"Sure. First you need a quick tour of the house, though, okay?"

Darlene readily agreed to that plan, and time passed quickly while the two young women caught up on news and discussed their men. Darlene told Polly about her college classes, the new roommate who had loaned her a car for the weekend, and her hopes that she and Jake might be able to set a wedding date in the near future. Polly was thrilled with the thought that Darlene and Jake might soon be settled in the area.

The telephone interrupted their work. Darlene stirred the cheese sauce while Polly went to the living room to pick up the phone.

Within five minutes, Polly returned and gave Darlene a hug. "Peter says Jake is on the ground and debriefing. They'll be here by six. I bet you can hardly wait!"

"I can hardly believe it, to be honest. The idea of seeing Jake here doesn't seem quite real yet."

"It's real all right. It is so neat how it worked out for him to go to Red Flag and stop here to see you on the way."

Darlene smiled diffidently. "He would have to come here anyway. The jets almost always come through Seymour

Johnson on the way to Nellis Air Force Base. Has Peter ever been to Red Flag? What exactly is it?"

"It's a training exercise held near Las Vegas. They go up against all kinds of other jets and pretend they're in a real war. I guess it's difficult and complicated, but excellent training for the flight crews. Peter went a few years ago, but not since we've been married."

The table was set, dinner was keeping warm in the oven, and Darlene was sitting on the floor, playing with little Drew, when Polly heard Peter's car pull into the garage. "They're home!" she announced, oblivious to Darlene's attack of the jitters.

Peter entered through the kitchen door, still talking with Jake. "Yeah, I want to put shelves up over there, but I haven't had the time yet," he said over his shoulder, then turned to embrace his wife. "Hi, honey. That's Darlene's car in the driveway?"

"Yup." Polly returned her husband's kiss. "She got here around three-thirty, and we've been gabbing nonstop ever since. Hello Jake! Welcome to North Carolina."

Jake stepped into the doorway behind Peter, looking somewhat ill at ease. "Thanks, Polly. Good to see you again." His dark hair was still damp and slicked back from his recent shower. Polly saw his eyes slide past her to where Darlene appeared in the kitchen doorway with Drew on one hip.

"Hmm. I'll come with you while you clean up, Peter, and leave these two to get reacquainted for a minute," Polly decided, taking her son from Darlene with a knowing grin. "Relax," she whispered in passing.

Darlene gave her a quick smile, then turned back to Jake. Strange how shy she felt; it had only been a few months since she'd last seen him.

Alone in the kitchen, they smiled at each other, then Jake opened his arms and wiggled his fingers. "Hug?"

Without hesitation she flew into his arms. "Oh, Jake! I can

hardly believe you're here!"

"Me neither. This has to be the longest day of my life. It would have been bad enough making that flight, but knowing I'd see you once I got here made it last forever."

She reached up to stroke his smooth cheek. "You look so tired. Do you feel all right?"

"Not the greatest, but holding you is doing wonders for me." He squeezed her tighter. "You look gorgeous, Darlene."

"Even with no pink leather?"

He chuckled. "Can't say I miss it. This sky-blue sweater is pretty."

"You like it? It's cashmere. Maria, my roommate, helped me pick this one out. Her taste is better than my last roommate's."

"Thankfully." He stole a quick kiss, then a longer one. Darlene buried her face in his neck, and they rocked slowly back and forth. "This is nice," he murmured into her hair. "I can't tell you how much I've missed you."

She nodded. "I know. It's always like part of me is missing. . .until now."

❧

After dinner, the two couples sat around the table and talked, discussing Jake's flight and the upcoming Red Flag exercise. When the men's subject matter became too technical, Polly and Darlene branched off into their own conversation about babies, and Darlene fed Drew his bedtime bottle.

Peter and Jake chuckled, reengaging the women's interest. "What's so funny?" Polly demanded, looking from one man to the other.

"Jake's pilot lost one shoe from each pair out of his baggage today," Peter explained.

"And his underwear," Jake added. "He acquired a cargo of rocks in exchange."

"What? How did that happen?" Polly demanded. "Did you do it, Jake?"

Jake lifted his hands. "I plead innocent. The culprits were some of the guys who didn't get to come to Red Flag. Hoss was too green to know better than to bring his bags into the squadron and leave them unattended while we briefed for the flight, so he got his stuff looted. It happened to me once, during a cross-country to Germany, but I only got my shoes taken, not my underwear. I learned never to bring my bags in until time to load them on the jet."

"Poor Hoss," Darlene sympathized. "Is he a good pilot?"

"Not bad. He's learning quickly. We talked a lot during the flight over today; I never knew him very well before. He's a good guy."

Polly suggested that they move to more comfortable seats in the living room. She put Drew to bed while Darlene served dessert and coffee to the still-talking men. After the dishes had been cleared, Darlene settled beside Jake on the couch and nestled beneath his arm. A large tabby cat lay sprawled across Peter's lap. The men were talking about Red Flag again; Peter was using his hands to illustrate an air-to-air combat tactic. Each time he absently petted the dozing cat between "sorties," a loud purr rumbled through the room.

Polly entered quietly and sat near her husband. After a few more spiels of technical jargon, she smiled at Darlene across the room and gave her a little wink, as if to say, "Get used to this."

"So what did you do during all that time in the air today? Take a nap?" Darlene asked Jake at the first opportunity.

Jake shook his head. "I needed to stay awake if only to make sure my pilot stayed awake. There wasn't much of anything to do but twiddle our thumbs; the tankers we traveled with did all the radio calls and planning from the time we took off till we were about one hundred miles from Seymour. Basically, we fly like tankers, not fighters, during a transatlantic flight. We air-refueled six times, but that was about the only excitement during the whole trip."

"I can't imagine sitting for ten hours straight without being able to get up or stretch out. Doesn't it drive you crazy?"

"It isn't much fun. I'm kinda numb in the backside, if you want to know the truth. This is the one time I rather envy the tanker crews."

"Do you wish you were flying 'heavies'?" Darlene asked.

Both men considered this for half a moment, then agreed in chorus, "Nah!" shaking their heads.

"Even if you could be pilot of a tanker?" Darlene questioned Jake further.

He still shook his head. "Nope. I like what I do. I'm content. To be honest, there are days when I wonder why, but they don't come often."

"You mean like when you get crewed with a. . .shall we say 'inept' pilot?" Peter prompted.

"You might say that." Jake grinned. "Have anyone in mind?"

"No names now," Polly admonished the men.

"Of course not," Peter looked affronted. "Wouldn't think of mentioning poor old—"

"Peter!"

He chuckled. "Did you ever hear the story of the 'learner' pilot, Darlene?"

She shook her head. "But I'd like to hear it."

"Well, there was one pilot—who shall remain nameless," he assured his wife, "who was the bane of Wizzos. He scared his backseaters out of their wits. One of our more experienced instructor Wizzos, Kevin Morris, was finally given the dirty job of 'retraining' him. Morris did his best, but one day when they came back from a hair-raising mission, the pilot made what we call a 'carrier landing,' meaning it was hard and fast, the way navy jets land on aircraft carriers."

"There's no need to land like that on a normal runway," Polly interjected.

"No, of course not. It's hard on the landing gear. Anyway,

after that landing, Morris held up a sign on the side of the cockpit where everyone but the pilot could see it: a white *L* on a red background, the 'learner' or 'student driver' sign in the United Kingdom."

"Oh, I remember those," Darlene said and chuckled. "Did the pilot find out?"

Both men laughed. "He couldn't help noticing how everyone he taxied past busted up laughing. He wasn't happy when he found out, but he couldn't stay mad; he knew he deserved the ribbing. To give him credit, he became a decent pilot eventually," Peter added.

"Morris has a screwy sense of humor. He's almost legendary around the Panther squadron," Jake commented.

"How's Chantel Morris doing?" Polly asked innocently. "She must have had her baby by now. Did you ever hear whether they had a boy or a girl?"

"I think I heard it was another girl," Jake answered slowly.

"Oh, that's nice. Their first baby girl was an absolute doll." Polly stopped and glanced from her husband's face to Jake's. "What's wrong?"

Peter sighed. "Don't like to gossip, but you're bound to hear before long. Chantel left Kevin, took the children, and moved back in with her parents."

Polly looked stunned. "Oh. Oh, I'm so sorry!"

Darlene reached to hold her hand. She hadn't known Chantel Morris personally, but she was aware that Polly had worked to develop a friendship with the wife of her former boyfriend. Kevin had married Chantel suddenly right after Polly married Peter, and everyone but Chantel had known that it was a rebound marriage. Now, apparently, the shaky marriage had crumbled.

There was silence for a long moment. "We need to pray for them both," Peter stated. "There is still hope for reconciliation. God can mend broken homes."

The four of them held hands in a circle and prayed for the

Morris family. Polly began to cry, and after the final amen, she excused herself to find a box of tissues. A quiet, contemplative mood hung over them, then Darlene saw Jake try to shake himself awake. She slipped her arm through his and rested her head on his shoulder. "Are you all right?"

"Yeah, just tired out. I'm sorry this thing about the Morrises came up tonight," Jake said softly, patting her hand. "Didn't mean to bring up a painful subject. Maybe I'd better go back to the hotel now and let all of us get some 'west and wewaxation.' "

"What's your schedule tomorrow, Elmer Fudd?" Darlene asked.

He smiled, resting his head against hers. "I have the day free until four o'clock, when we've got a briefing. We check out of the motel Saturday morning at eight, then it's off to Las Vegas. Do you have plans for tomorrow?"

"Just to be with you. Maybe we could have a picnic in the park or go for a drive."

"I can't go far from the base, but the picnic sounds good."

❧

The next day, Jake and Darlene picked up a lunch at a local delicatessen and managed to locate Herman Park. It was a cool, windy, late October day, and few mothers had brought their children to the playground. No matter the weather, Jake and Darlene carried their sunshine with them. Both of them kept breaking into smiles at the slightest provocation or for no particular reason at all.

Darlene laid out the luncheon, anchoring their plates with food and the stack of napkins with her purse. "You're feeling better this morning?" she inquired after Jake asked the blessing.

"Yes, much better, thanks. Sorry I was a dud last night. Here all I could think of during that entire flight was how I would get to see you soon, and then when we were together I was too tired to really enjoy it. I know I talked too much, but

I can't even remember what I talked about!"

Darlene reached across the picnic table to hold his hand. "Don't worry about it, Jake. It was probably a good thing the party broke up when it did. We'll enjoy today more since you got a good night's sleep. I think this is your sandwich, turkey and jack cheese on rye."

Jake opened his fruit drink and took a swig, then twirled the bottle on the vinyl tablecloth. "Darlene, I have some news."

She stopped distributing the potato chips between their plates. "Oh? Good or bad?"

"Good." He grinned. "Very good. I got the job here at Seymour in the 334th Fighter Squadron as an instructor Wizzo. My report date is January twentieth."

"Oh, Jake, that's wonderful! Does this mean we can—?" She stopped, flushed, and tried again. "I mean, what now? With your plans, I mean. . ."

"Our plans, you mean," he interrupted gently. "Don't be embarrassed, sweetheart. I know exactly what you're thinking—the same thing I'm thinking. How soon can we be married?"

She nodded shyly. "But you haven't. . .we're not. . ."

"Will you marry me, Darlene?"

She nodded again. "Yes."

They stared at each other across the table. "There. Now we're engaged," Jake stated with a teasing grin. "Want to look at rings?"

"Soon as we're done eating," she agreed enthusiastically. "When can we get married? During Christmas break?"

"Sounds good to me. I don't want to be separated again right after we get married, but I know you have to be back at school before I report for work at this base. I have plenty of leave time built up, so we'll work something out. We've got to find a reasonable place to live, too. Somewhere midway between the base and the college."

"Can we ship François here?" she asked anxiously. "I

know it's expensive, but I really miss my dog."

"What's a home without a dog? Of course we'll keep him."

"Thank you! Oh, Jake, this is so exciting! I can hardly believe this is happening!" Her head cocked to one side. "Don't you want to kiss me?"

He chuckled. "Come on over here. Can't kiss you across the table."

❧

They were too excited to eat much. Later, at a jewelry store in the mall, Darlene picked out a dainty solitaire diamond on a simple gold band, and Jake paid cash for it on the spot. "I came prepared, you see," he admitted, watching his fiancée admire her ring.

"I'm so glad you did! You're always prepared for anything, Jake," she told him, exaggerating freely. "We need to call our parents. Oh, by the way, I forgot to tell you about the letter your mother, Mrs. Edgewood, sent me a few weeks ago."

"Oh, yeah? I gave her your address, but I didn't know she had written to you already. What did she say?" Jake took her arm as they strolled down the mall.

"It was the sweetest letter! She told me a lot of things about you as a boy that amazed me. She also told me that Teri has a serious relationship with a man she's known for years but would never consider as a possible husband until now. They plan to go to Peru as missionaries. Isn't that neat? Anyway, I know your mother had her heart set on you marrying Teri, so it was awfully good of her to be so kind to me, a total stranger."

"Actually, I think she had given up on my marrying anyone; you came as a welcome surprise. So. . .what 'things' did she tell you about me?" His black brows pulled together in a slightly worried frown.

"Oh, she told me about how wild you were when you first came to Sunday school. Did you really have a foul mouth? And did you really smoke? I found all that very hard to believe. I mean, I know the Lord can change people from the inside out, but a wild boy like that. . ." She shook her head. "It's amazing!"

Jake shook his head. "Can't say I'm glad she told you all that junk, but I guess you need to know. Yeah, I was about as wild as an eleven-year-old boy can be, the horror of several foster families. I don't know what Dad Edgewood saw in me when I visited their Sunday school class, but I was starved for a father's love, and he wanted a son. He was the father I had always dreamed of having, and he tells me I'm the son he had always dreamed of having. He led me to the Lord that summer, and they adopted me the next year. The rest, as they say, is history."

Jake stopped, took Darlene by the arms, and looked into her eyes. "I had a lousy childhood until the Edgewoods came along, but my heart's desire is to have a home like yours—a strong marriage, children raised with love and discipline, financial security, and above all, the Lord in control. I would never abuse you in any way; you are the greatest treasure of my earthly life, second only to my Lord."

Darlene swallowed hard and blinked back sudden tears. "You're one of the gentlest, most considerate people I've ever known, Jake. I think maybe the hardship and evil you've experienced have made you more appreciative of the blessings and joy you now possess and more determined never to lose them. I know you're not perfect, but I believe you're the man who will make me a happy woman for the rest of my life." Her face glowed with sincerity and love.

"In the Lord's strength, I'll do my best!" Jake took her left hand, admired the new ring, tucked her hand under his arm, and started back down the mall, smiling contentedly.

Darlene laid her head on his shoulder and hugged his arm close, her eyes brighter than the diamond on her finger. "To think, all this started because of a traffic accident!"

epilogue

It happened at the wedding rehearsal, during the second trial run. The mothers had just been seated by two nervous ushers, Reg Sutton and Derrick Althorp. Reverend Blake Grenfell entered the sanctuary from the side door, followed closely by Jake and his best man, Pete Shackleton. Rustling, whispering, and a few giggles came from the back of the church, where the matron of honor, Danielle Althorp Grenfell, practiced her steps and Darlene clung to her father's brawny arm.

From her seat on the bride's side of the church, Dora bluntly told her future son-in-law, "Now you mustn't look so nervous when Darlene walks down the aisle toward you, Josiah Kyle. People will think Don is holding a shotgun to your back."

"Why would they think that when he'll be right beside Darlene?" Jake returned, trying not to be irritated. He paused, his eyes widening, then blurted, "Someone told you!"

"Pardon?" Dora stared at him in confusion. "Someone told me what?"

"My name! They must have."

Her jaw dropped. "You mean. . . ?"

"I didn't even let Darlene put it on the invitations, but you found out. It was Mom who told you, wasn't it?"

"I never said a word," poor Beverly Edgewood protested from her seat on the groom's side of the church. "I wouldn't dare, after all the warnings I've been given. Leigh and Reg threatened me with all manner of dire repercussions if I should dare call my son by his real name." She shook her head in calm resignation.

Reverend Blake glanced from his mother-in-law to his future brother-in-law and back again, looking rather befuddled. "I'm afraid I'm not following this conversation very well."

"Oh, it's a long story." Dora chuckled, then frowned thoughtfully at Jake and added, "Now which name did I just call you? I've forgotten!"

A Letter To Our Readers

Dear Reader:

In order that we might better contribute to your reading enjoyment, we would appreciate your taking a few minutes to respond to the following questions. When completed, please return to the following:

Rebecca Germany, Managing Editor
Heartsong Presents
P.O. Box 719
Uhrichsville, Ohio 44683

1. Did you enjoy reading *Finally, Love?*
   ❏ Very much. I would like to see more books by this author!
   ❏ Moderately
   I would have enjoyed it more if _____

   _____

2. Are you a member of **Heartsong Presents**? ❏Yes ❏No
   If no, where did you purchase this book? _____

   _____

3. What influenced your decision to purchase this book? (Check those that apply.)

   ❏ Cover   ❏ Back cover copy

   ❏ Title   ❏ Friends

   ❏ Publicity   ❏ Other_____

4. How would you rate, on a scale from 1 (poor) to 5 (superior), the cover design? _____

5. On a scale from 1 (poor) to 10 (superior), please rate the following elements.

    ___Heroine   ___Plot

    ___Hero   ___Inspirational theme

    ___Setting   ___Secondary characters

6. What settings would you like to see covered in **Heartsong Presents** books?_____

_____

_____

7. What are some inspirational themes you would like to see treated in future books?_____

_____

_____

8. Would you be interested in reading other **Heartsong Presents** titles?   ❑ Yes   ❑ No

9. Please check your age range:
  ❑ Under 18   ❑ 18-24   ❑ 25-34
  ❑ 35-45   ❑ 46-55   ❑ Over 55

10. How many hours per week do you read? _____

Name _____

Occupation _____

Address _____

City_____ State_____ Zip_____

WHEN I'M ON MY KNEES

Anita Corrine Donihue

Prayers especially for women, prayers that emanate from
the heart, prayers that deal with friendship, family, and
peace. Packaged in a beautifully printed leatherette cover,
women will also find hymns and poems that focus
on prayer in their everyday lives.

About the author:
Anita Corrine Donihue, a teacher with thirty years
of experience, is the coauthor of *Apples for a Teacher*
and *Joy to the World,* two very popular titles
from Barbour Books.

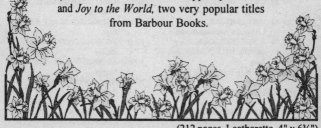

(212 pages, Leatherette, 4" x 6¾")

Heartsong Presents
Love Stories Are Rated G!

That's for godly, gratifying, and of course, great! If you love a thrilling love story, but don't appreciate the sordidness of some popular paperback romances, **Heartsong Presents** is for you. In fact, **Heartsong Presents** is the *only inspirational romance book club*, the only one featuring love stories where Christian faith is the primary ingredient in a marriage relationship.

Sign up today to receive your first set of four, never before published Christian romances. Send no money now; you will receive a bill with the first shipment. You may cancel at any time without obligation, and if you aren't completely satisfied with any selection, you may return the books for an immediate refund!

Imagine. . .four new romances every four weeks—two historical, two contemporary—with men and women like you who long to meet the one God has chosen as the love of their lives. . .all for the low price of $9.97 postpaid.

To join, simply complete the coupon below and mail to the address provided. **Heartsong Presents** romances are rated G for another reason: They'll arrive *Godspeed!*